Allachburn

Thank you for looking
after me so well.

Gerald Hammond

Xmas 2,013

The Goods

Chas (never Charles) Gowans, university drop out and drug addict, lived on the fringes of the underworld and supplemented his unemployment benefit with petty theft and dubious chores to support his habit. His lover, Sylvia, detested his drug-taking and he had to conceal from her his growing dependence and the ever-increasing costs.

It was the expense which forced him to accept the driving job for The Irishman. He was to deliver seven suitcases to London. Chas knew they were bombs, but he took the job all the same. If he kept quiet there would be more well paid jobs. What he hadn't bargained for was Sylvia witnessing The Irishman's involvement. She had to be removed, so he decided to sell her and make a profit out of catastrophe.

The consequent sequence of events is complex: sometimes farcical; sometimes frightening; always gripping. As the story races to an explosive but satisfactory conclusion Arthur Douglas presents us with a host of lively characters.

A perfectly plotted and superbly satisfying thriller.

Arthur Douglas

THE GOODS

MACMILLAN

First published 1985 by
MACMILLAN LONDON LIMITED
4 Little Essex Street London WC2R 3LF
and Basingstoke

Associated companies in Auckland, Delhi, Dublin, Gaborone, Hamburg, Harare, Hong Kong, Johannesburg, Kuala Lumpur, Lagos, Manzini, Melbourne, Mexico City, Nairobi, New York, Singapore and Tokyo

Typeset by Bookworm Typesetting Ltd
Printed and bound in Great Britain by
Anchor Brendon Ltd, Tiptree, Essex

British Library Cataloguing in Publication Data
Douglas, Arthur, *1926-*
The goods.
I. Title
823′.914[F]   PR6054.082

ISBN 0-333-39757-6

ONE

The Oaken Tree was incongruous for the heart of a small, industrial city – an old coaching inn, perfect and unspoiled. Somehow it had escaped the hazards of subsidence and rot, of falling bombs or rising damp or developers' bids. It had even escaped the depredations of managements. It had neither been modernised with gaming machines and piped music nor cosied up with fake and improbable antiques. It remained what it had always been, a harmonious and mildly unfashionable place of refreshment. Most of its clientèle liked it without knowing the reason. They were not the sort of people to wonder why.

The young couple in the corner could have passed for brother and sister, but they were not related by anything more than a precarious affair. They had the same dark hair and lean build although the girl was naturally broader of hip and fuller of bosom. Each had the intense, nervous features which often proclaim the student, and each wore the student uniform of long hair, jeans and loose sweater, so that it took a second glance at hip or chin or chest to determine which was the boy and which was the girl.

To a casual glance, their expressions might also have passed for identical. But the girl's face, full-lipped and wide-eyed, was in the mould on which contentment would rest easily. Her discontent was superficial, no more than regret over a dying dream allied to the natural contempt of youth for a world which was unsatisfactory and for which it could still pass the blame. The boy's anger lay deeper.

Sylvia Cantor and Chas (never Charles) Gowans had known each other, in every sense including the biblical, at the local university which, although of the reddest brick, took itself seriously as a seat of learning. The liberated Miss Cantor had accepted Chas as a lover until, under pressure from the disenchanted authorities, he had dropped out. Sylvia had stayed to take her mediocre degree and to be taken, several times, by a handsome young army officer on leave from his unit in Northern Ireland.

She had not pined for Chas. His, she knew, had been little more than a physical need, hers a response to that need and an act of defiance. But when, by chance, they had met again in the queue for a pop concert, there had been a trace of old magic to re-awaken, with the ease of established precedent and the tickle of the biological urge. Within a few minutes, he had asked her to move in with him.

A week later, but circumspectly, she did so. Her officer had returned to his unit without entering into any commitment and home was deadly dull. Her parents had seemed to accept her story of a walking tour with a girlfriend. They could still love their daughter but, unemployed and in rebellious mood, she was not nice to have underfoot.

That had been a month ago.

Chas took a pull at his beer. 'Going to be make-your-mind-up time soon,' he said.

Sylvia nodded and keyed up the date on Chas's cheap digital watch. 'Rosie'll be back in another eight days,' she said. After that, their affair was over or out in the open.

'So what'll you do?'

'For the umpteenth time, I don't know!' Home, comfort and security held out an attraction, but so also did the gesture of living openly as a drop out's mistress. If she gave home another try, would she now be able to control her temper when her parents bumbled in their well-meaning way? Or, if she threw in her lot with Chas, would she have any control over his darker side? He was not the man that she had thought she remembered. He was not even the same mildly vigorous lover.

Once, they had been able to discuss anything. Now, Chas would have declared certain subjects taboo. Risking his wrath, she re-opened one of them. 'I'll stay,' she said, 'if you'll give up taking that stuff. Or if you'll promise to try.'

Chas controlled his irritation with a visible effort. 'It does something for me,' he said coldly. 'You can't understand. If you had any idea what you were talking about, I might listen to you. If you'd tried it for yourself . . . '

She shivered. 'Not me!' she said. 'I don't mind sharing a joint at a party. That's because I don't feel bad while it's wearing off and I know I won't care how long it is before I touch another one. But that hard stuff . . . I've seen you coming out of it, Chas. And my dad says that once you start mainlining, your days are numbered.'

'So don't mainline,' he said. 'There's no need for it.' She couldn't bear to watch him taking his medicine, as he called it. She had no idea that he was already shooting direct into a vein. His addiction was much further advanced that either of them allowed her to believe. 'What does your dad think he is? What does he know?'

'I used to think he didn't know much,' she said with a spark of humour. 'Now I'm surprised how much he's learned. Chas, please, couldn't you kick it? Not all at once, but slowly. There are places . . . '

She was getting under his skin, telling him things which he had told himself in the past but which, he was sure, were now too late or beyond his strength. He opened his mouth to snap at her and she braced herself for what was coming. They were both glad of the interruption.

It came in the form of The Irishman – as he was often called, setting him far apart from any other Hibernian in the district. Locally he answered to the name of Sean O'Connell, although he had been born Wilf Connors and had used a dozen other names besides.

Sylvia was inclined to set store by personal appearance and would have indulged her own taste for pretty clothes and careful hairdressing if these had not been the hallmarks of the despised bourgeoisie. She liked to see a man who cared for his turnout. The Irishman, despite an ingratiating manner, failed to impress her. His hair, which should have been the colour of dull copper, was dark with its own grease and spilled dandruff on to an equally greasy anorak. His bow legs hinted at a horsey background – although he smelled, she thought, of almost everything but horses – but in conjunction with a hollow chest they pointed more strongly to an undernourished childhood. In theory, she should have loved him for his poor beginnings, but although she might sway to the left she was in no danger of falling.

'Hullo there, young Chas,' was his greeting. 'Are you not going to buy an old pal a drink and introduce him to your dolly bird then?'

Chas performed a grudging introduction and went to the bar for a Bushmills. The Irishman lowered himself into a spare chair. Sylvia leaned away. His breath already smelled of whisky and he was articulating with more than normal care. 'Sylvia, is it? "Who is Sylvia, what is she?" I remember that from school. A darling name. I had a sister of that name once. Maybe I still have, back in the Old Country.'

'That's nice,' Sylvia said without conviction.

'Nice, yes. Nice that she's there and I'm here. A right

ratbag she is, and always was.'

'Oh?'

'That's so. We think she may have had an English father.'

Chas came back with a tray holding the Bushmills and another pint for himself. Sylvia was left to nurse the remnant of her lager and lime.

The Irishman sank his Irish whiskey, nodded politely to Sylvia and got to his feet. 'A fine girl,' he said. 'I may ask you for a lend of her some time.' He waited, as if for an answer, got none, nodded again and wandered away.

'I hate professional provincials,' Sylvia said moodily, 'like Eh-ba-goom Yorkshiremen and Harry Lauder-type Scots. I thought he was going to call me Acushla and produce a shillelagh. And he's weird. Isn't he?'

'You'd better believe it,' Chas said. 'Just don't say it aloud. Not where he can hear you. He's a nutter.'

'So why don't you tell him to go forth and multiply, or words to that effect?'

'Listen,' Chas said earnestly, 'The Irishman is one person you do not tell to fuck off. He may not look it, but that is one hard man, but hard. Fat Alec was telling me.'

Sylvia wrinkled her nose. 'I wouldn't believe that man if I knew he was telling the truth.'

'This is true enough. I've heard it all over. The Irishman put a man in hospital just for telling a joke about the pope.'

'He's from the south then?' Sylvia asked. She disliked The Irishman but she was intrigued by hard men.

'He's IRA, that much I do know,' Chas said. 'If you ever meet him again, keep off the subject of the Troubles. Once he starts laying off about Partition there's no stopping him. Everything from Oliver Cromwell to "D" Block in the Maze. And all second-hand stuff. It isn't as if he even understood what he's talking about. That's the most dangerous type, the fanatic who doesn't understand his own cause. You can respect a man who's fanatical out of his own convictions. But the fanatic who's been brought up to believe unthinkingly any doctrine, from a religion to a political party, scares me. Because he may be wrong but he's not capable of wondering.'

'I don't understand any of them,' Sylvia said. 'Good Catholics and Protestants killing and maiming each other in the name of their churches and supposed to be trying to unite themselves. It's all contradictions in terms. No wonder the Irish are supposed to be mad.'

'They're supposed to be mad because they are bloody mad. Their fight isn't about religion, nor about union. The fight's between north and south and it goes back to long before any of the things they say they're fighting about. The real reasons are lost and forgotten. But, being Irish, they have to fight about some damn thing and if it wasn't this it'd be something else. Last war, there was more than one Irish family had sons fighting on both sides. They're all mad, it's just that some are madder than others. Fat Alec says that The Irishman could have retired in comfort years ago if he didn't waste most of his time and money on the IRA.'

'What does he do for a living?'

'That I don't know. Fat Alec hinted that he was a crook, but bloody good at whatever it is that he does. So if you meet him again stay polite but don't get involved.'

'What would you do if he did ask for a loan of me?' Sylvia asked. The idea was squalid and yet she could not resist toying with it. 'Would you stand up to him?'

'I think he was only needling me. But maybe we'd better change our pub. He's in here a lot.'

'There's been a lot about the IRA in the papers recently.'

'Such as what?' Chas never read the papers. He said that he had done enough reading as a student to last him a lifetime.

'They're threatening a new wave of bombings in British cities unless some of their key men are let out of the Maze.'

'Bastards!' Chas said. 'You're not safe anywhere these days. Except . . . maybe we'll do our drinking here after all. He'd never bomb his own local.'

'You think he might be a bomber for the IRA?'

'I don't know. I wouldn't want to count on him not being. He's mad enough.'

Already Chas, who rarely even pretended to be endowed with courage, was balancing in his mind the relative dangers. He decided that if The Irishman asked for a loan of Sylvia, a loan he would get.

Fat Alec was not so much fat as broad. Although a small roll of fat overhung the waist-band on a stomach whose muscles were sagging with middle age, the impression of grossness sprang from a heavy frame, heavily muscled. But he liked to be thought of as having the soft ineffectiveness of the fat man. In a dangerous profession, it is safer to be dangerous while those around you think you safe.

He was a careful man, walking softly for all his bulk, always in the shadows. A short childhood in one of Britain's toughest slums had taught him the virtue of caution and his present status had cemented the knowledge. Between those extremes he had spent thirty years clawing his way up many ladders, eliminating his rivals by guile rather than violence. He could fight effectively and ruthlessly if pushed, but if violence was only a matter of policy he preferred to pay others to be violent on his behalf. As the premier pusher on his chosen territory he could live in comparative peace and plenty as long as he stayed out of the limelight.

He had his regular customers. (The casual seeker after marijuana to boost a swinging party dealt only with one or other of his part-time agents.) But he avoided in his habits any regularity which might be noticed by the Drugs Squad. His places of business, which were many, changed from hour to hour and he never repeated their sequence or timing. Any client missing an appointment could hunt for him as an alternative to waiting for days until the same meeting place was scheduled for another visit. He could count on any of them being desperate enough to find him somehow. He could also count on their discretion. He warned them regularly of the consequences of a careless word. Occasionally, he used The Irishman as his stick to beat the dog, and he made a point of embellishing the man's reputation for violence.

Chas was a few minutes late for his appointment. He had had difficulty leaving Sylvia behind. The girl was beginning to cling. But she would have been both shocked and inquisitive if she had seen the price and scale of his purchase. To his relief, Fat Alec was waiting patiently, kneeling in the back pew of a small and empty church. The pusher knew well that addicts rarely ran to time, so he allowed a margin between customers.

The church was not Catholic. Not that Alec had anything against the Catholics, but he had a profound distrust of confessional boxes. Once, when checking the booths for lurking clergy or lingering penitents, he had found a priest in residence and expectant for his confession. For once in his life, his mind had gone blank. He would have run for it, except that it was against his instincts to draw attention to himself. Worse, he was expecting a customer. In his confusion he might even have made a true confession, but he recovered at least a part of his wits in time. Unable to think of anything more innocuous, he scrambled together a story about having lustful thoughts towards his neighbour's wife, but remembering the hideousness of his neighbour's wife he made a last-minute substitution of the lady's cherished

Labrador retriever. The scandalised priest had imposed a penance which, if the pusher had cared to implement it and had known how, would have taken him a month. Still shaking, Fat Alec had intercepted his next customer, a commercial artist with a local agency, in the church porch and had thereafter avoided any establishment higher than Anglican.

The pusher seemed to have dozed off. Chas knelt down at his side and gave him a nudge. Fat Alec yawned and his eyes opened. 'The usual?' he whispered.

Chas nodded. His usual order was barely enough to last him the week now and he would dearly have loved to increase it. He could have explained the increase to himself as a reserve against the day when Sylvia would weaken. But his faculty for self-criticism had not yet died and he knew that he would inevitably give in and enlarge his own dosage.

Fat Alec nodded and opened a hymnal. 'Hundred and eighty,' he said.

'Hundred and thirty,' Chas reminded him.

'It's gone up.'

'Christ, I can't pay that!'

'Keep your voice down. You're in the house of God.' Fat Alec was not wholly without humour. 'If you can't pay, go short. Or lift another telly off a pensioner.'

'If I did, I couldn't sell it until Monday. Give me half my usual and meet me in three days.'

'I'm not splitting a packet here.'

Chas was out and he had begun to sweat. Soon his nose would run and he would feel the spiders in his hair. Then the cramps would begin, but there was still a vestige of strength in him. 'I think I'll shop around a bit. Take competitive quotations, like. Just in case you're the lowest tenderer, where'll you be this time tomorrow?'

He started to get up but Fat Alec caught his sleeve and pulled him down again. The price had genuinely risen, due to the law of supply and demand and the seizure of a large consignment at Hull. The pusher was adding something for himself; not solely out of greed but because Chas was the least untrustworthy of his clients and there was a job he wanted done. But if a regular customer like Chas went shopping for another source, word might get back and the bosses would ask questions.

'Special discount for a favoured customer,' Fat Alec whispered. 'To you, just this once, a hundred and sixty.'

'I only got a hundred and a half, and I still got the rent to pay.'

'The rent can wait. I bet you can't.'

'The rent can't wait either. They're holding their breaths for an excuse to evict me.'

'You got a problem, son.' Inside his barrel-shaped chest, the pusher was laughing. Even at the right price it was going to be all right. 'You can drive a car, can't you?'

'Of course.' Chas might not have a valid licence, but he could drive.

'You want to earn a quick two hundred?'

It was barely a question. Chas was supporting himself, his girl and his habit by the theft of televisions, videos and home computers from families rash enough to leave their homes empty. But, as an occupation, it was hard on the nerves. Several times he had been interrupted and had resorted to his fists to escape. Already he suspected that the police had his description and were watching for him. The pitcher could go too often to the well. 'What would I have to do?' he asked.

'Go and talk to The Irishman.'

'I might be too busy looking for another supplier.'

Fat Alec sighed. He hated to give credit. He slipped a plastic envelope between the pages of the hymnal and passed it over. 'Hundred and fifty now, you owe me ten and you get the rent off The Irishman. Next week, same day, eleven thirty in the aquarium at the zoo. Hundred and eighty plus the ten you owe me.'

'All right,' Chas said despondently.

Fat Alec looked round. A woman, dressed in shiny black under a cheap fur, had entered the church. 'Now bugger off,' he whispered. 'I got another worshipper to bless.'

The Irishman was hard at work in the lock-up garage which, despite his lack of a car, he rented from the council. He paid an extra rent because some previous tenant had installed a supply of electricity.

Wilf Connors' direction in life had been pre-ordained. He had been born into an impoverished family in a small but fanatical Catholic enclave in Belfast. The family was poor, not because of any lack of skills or opportunity but because, already setting the pattern for their son to follow a generation later, his parents preferred to expend their energy and resources in the interests of the Cause, leaving such matters as food and clothing to the spasmodic generosity of neighbours.

Belief in the infallibility of the IRA and the divine right of its activist limbs were basic tenets of existence, as unquestionable as the existence of the street outside. The lack of any right on the part of the Protestant majority to advance any counter-argument was equally certain. By his tenth birthday there was no room in young Wilf's mind for any other creed but hatred and destruction. His father had gone south to fight the Black and Tans in the streets of Dublin. His elder brothers, finding the Maze prison less uncomfortable than their own home, gave it their regular patronage. His sisters gave aid and comfort in many forms to the terrorists, starting by carrying weapons to and from the scenes of shootings in their school satchels.

It had been a family decision that Wilf was destined for greater things than street soldiery. Having shown an early aptitude for things electrical and mechanical, he was apprenticed to his Uncle Bob in Omagh. Together, by day, they ran a radio and TV repair shop, but outside of business hours Wilf was taught the art of the bomber by his uncle, who had himself learned his skills from the great Tom Gallagher. At one time, after a particularly successful series of counter-measures by the UDR, they had been the sole supplier of explosive devices for more than six months.

Wilf Connors had received a thorough grounding in explosives. He learned how to buy, steal, or, in emergencies, to make them. He learned their handling, in safety to the handler and with the maximum danger to the enemy, from dynamite and gelignite to the later, more dependable and more violent, plastics. He learned to activate bombs by a variety of timing devices and to protect them against disarming by others. As the technical war developed, he learned to rig the notorious milk-churn bomb to explode as the chosen target passed by, first by remote cable and then by radio.

The battle of wits accelerated. Uncle Bob was left behind in the technological rush but Wilf, thanks to ever more advanced courses at the Technical College, emerged among the experts. The British learned to record the coded radio test signals and to play them back to the brief dismay of the bombers. Wilf was among the first to counter this perfidious trick by a switch of both code and wavelength between the test and the firing signal. For more than a year, he ran an underground night class above a bakery in Enniskillen.

But among his many faults was a mouth ever open for the intake of alcohol and the outflow of unguarded speech. He was also unable to resist the temptation to use his considerable skills for the opening of post office safes. Most of the proceeds went to support his activities or were given direct to Sinn Fein, but this was no excuse.

The country was too hot to hold him and his arrest would be only a matter of time. From an asset, he had become a liability.

A lesser man would have vanished, probably into Strangford Lough. It was not IRA gratitude which kept him alive – there is no room for gratitude in freedom fighting – but the fact that he might still have his uses as a consultant or as a manufacturer in the heart of the enemy's homeland. He was whisked across the Irish Sea and helped into the first of many changed identities. He was isolated from all sources of real information, forbidden to make personal contact with any of his new or former allies and approached only at long range and through expendable intermediaries.

His donations to the Cause could now be accepted or even welcomed without fear of betrayal by that loose tongue.

That afternooon, when Chas started to look for him, he was at work on two trestle tables stolen from the church hall. There was a great thirst on him, but he was firm with himself. He would do the work while he was still sober enough to trust his hands. It was good to be using his skills again, even if the present commission made no great technical demands on them. It was like riding a bicycle, he thought; you never forgot.

In each of eight, carefully dissimilar attaché cases he placed a cardboard box. Into each box, neat packets of RDX, four times more powerful even than plastique from the FN factory. As he fitted the timers – from the nearest Electricity Board showroom – he blessed the Cambridge scientists who had designed RDX and the ICI storeman who had, for a price, smuggled it out to him. None of the instability of the older explosives, the dangerous sweating, the nitroglycerine headaches. Round the cardboard boxes he packed plastic bags of nuts, bolts, washers and ball-bearings. He placed the primers, the batteries and an ingenious anti-tampering device of his own design and manufacture. Apart from the detonators, which he taped separately to the insides of the lids, all was ready.

He decided that he had earned a drink.

When Chas found him, The Irishman was propping up the bar and in expansive mood. He was regaling a group of regulars with a succession of Irish anecdotes. Although in theory he detested every Englishman and every Protestant, in practice he would have counted many English 'Proddies' among his best friends; and while he revered the Irish above all nations he was not blind to their faults. Yet, Chas noticed, while he could recognise mixed thinking among his compatriots he saw no signs of it in himself.

Chas contained his impatience, nursing a half pint and watching the clock behind the bar. He had had his fix, but months ago he had reached the stage at which drugs bought him little more than normality. At last he managed to catch The Irishman's eye.

They met at the corner of the bar.

'No dolly bird tonight?'

Chas shook his head. 'Fat Alec said to speak to you.'

'Sure, I thought that it might be yourself. Are you not going to buy an old pal a drink?' The last words were no more than a Pavlovian reflex.

'I'm broke,' Chas said. 'Fat Alec cleaned me out.'

Reluctantly, The Irishman forked out for another half pint and a Bushmills for himself. 'He does that sometimes,' he agreed. 'Well, we'll just have to see if we can't do something about it. This is just a small driving job, you understand. Take some parcels to London, ask nothing, say nothing, remember even less. Pays a hundred and fifty. You got a car?'

'I can get a car,' Chas said. He could always get a car.

One of the boyfriends of his elder sister had been an expert. 'Fat Alec said two hundred and expenses, which probably means it's worth more.'

'What expenses? I'm not giving you an expense account.'

'Petrol there, fare back,' Chas said. 'And my food.'

'You'd have to eat, wherever you were,' The Irishman pointed out. 'Two hundred. Fifty now and the rest in London. Plus your travelling costs. And that's the absolute top, take it or leave it. For that money I could send a taxi.'

'I'll take it,' Chas said quickly. 'Give me the fifty, I've got to run.'

'Come into the bog a minute, then,' The Irishman said. 'And bring the car to Berkshire Mews at noon tomorrow.'

TWO

In the small, concrete shopping centre which echoed to his footsteps, the rent office was about to close. The neighbouring shops had already shut but, Friday being both rent day and rates day, the rent office stayed open late. The rush of tenants, some obsequious and some threatening or querulous over dampness or outstanding repairs, was over. The girls were putting on coats and fluffing out their hair, readying themselves to meet their boys and make inroads into their own wages before their parents could get to them. The cashier was preparing to lock the day's takings in the strongroom.

'You, is it?' the cashier said. 'Not done a moonlight, then?' He stood barely five feet tall, but his job gave him a sense of power.

'Not this time,' Chas said. 'When I do, I'll send you a greetings telegram. And there's a minute to go. Here's my book.'

The cashier took his money and made change. 'One of these days you'll cut it too fine,' he said. 'And then you'll be out. You know there's an eviction order against you already. One non-payment, that's all it needs. The housing manager's waiting to pounce.'

'Maybe I should give him the chance he's waiting for. Then I'd be a homeless person and the council'd have to re-house me. They couldn't find me a grottier hole than the one I'm in now. I could just do with a nice little house with a bit of a garden.'

The cashier gave him back his rent book. 'I can just see you keeping a garden, I don't think.' He turned back to the strongroom. The girls started saying their good nights.

Business finished, Chas had time on his hands which he might just as well spend in needling his old enemy. Nobody loves the man who takes the rent. 'Don't tell me you leave that lot in the safe overnight,' he said incuriously. 'I'll have to save up for a tin opener.'

Over his shoulder, the cashier gave Chas what he fondly hoped was a piercing glance. 'Under these alarms . . . ' he waved a hand and a tiny red light glowed in a box on the wall ' . . . and with the cop shop just up the road, it's safer than carrying the money to the night safe. Specially with tearaways like you on the streets, just waiting for the chance to use a pick handle.'

'Quite right,' Chas said. 'Very sensible. Except that I wouldn't need a pick handle to deal with two-penn'orth of nothing like you. A feather duster would do the job nicely.'

One of the girls giggled.

'Why can't I come with you?' Sylvia asked disconsolately. 'I could just do with a trip to London. If you're being paid, we could have a meal and go to a show.'

'Well, you can't,' Chas said for the fourth time.

'What am I supposed to do here while you're away?' She swept her hand around the room.

To himself, Chas admitted that she had a point. The building was old but the decoration seemed to be the original and the furniture, much of which had been through the hands of the Salvation Army at least once, was no newer. The debris of careless housekeeping completed an unsavoury picture.

'You could try to tidy this dump up a bit,' he said. 'Even the flies are complaining.'

'And when I do try to clean the place up,' Sylvia said, 'you complain that you can't find anything and talk about petty bourgeois habits.'

'It'll only be for a few hours. Then I'll be back and I'll take you out.'

'To the pub,' Sylvia said, sniffing.

'Not the pub. Something to eat, somewhere nice, and the movies. Or I'll bring you back a present. Or both.' Chas was becoming desperate.

'But why . . . '

'Look, it's a chauffeuring job, for Christ's sake. The chap's lost his licence, got caught by the breathalyser. About ten thousand milligrams per millilitre, so they've banned him until he's too old to drive. He needs somebody to drive him to the Smoke and around. He wouldn't want the chauffeur bringing his tart along, would he?'

'I suppose not. And don't call me a tart. That's one thing I haven't sunk to yet.'

Chas just stopped himself from saying that if she were a tart she would be able to contribute to the housekeeping.

'It's just a word,' he said patiently. 'You called me a sod the other day.'

Sylvia smiled in spite of herself. 'With you, who can be sure?' she asked.

'You're always on at me to get a job. If he likes me, this could be the start of something regular.'

'I'll believe that when I see it,' Sylvia said, but she was softening. 'Do you really mean to give it a try?'

'Of course.' Chas shuffled his feet and moved towards the door.

'But a chauffeur!' Sylvia said. 'With your education, couldn't you do better?'

'As a chauffeur, I could be driving round in a Rolls. Using my education – which I never finished, remember – the best I'm likely to do is a clapped-out Mini.'

Sylvia frowned. There was a hole in his argument

somewhere. Chas made his escape before she could find it.

Sharp at noon, Chas drove a nearly new Rover into the mews. The car was in perfect order. The only defect which he could have pointed out would have been a broken latch on a quarter-light, which he had forced with a miniature crowbar. In a few more seconds he had found the right key from among his comprehensive collection and was on his way. It was the third car he had entered in the free car park, but the first with a full tank. Sylvia's regular lectures about the practice of economy were beginning to get to him.

The Irishman raised the door of a lock-up garage as he approached. Interpreting some vague gestures, Chas backed the car up to the doorway, got out and unlocked the boot. There was a pair of Zeiss binoculars in the boot and a good camera. Eight attaché cases were ranged on one of the tables in the garage. The Irishman lifted two of them into the boot. Chas put in two more and found them heavier than he had expected. The Irishman moved another two, stacking them carefully. Chas went for the last pair.

'Don't be so eager,' The Irishman said. 'One of them's my personal luggage.'

'Which one?'

'Doesn't matter.' The Irishman's voice was thick and unguarded.

'I put fifteen quid into the tank,' Chas said plaintively. 'And there's my fare home. By the time I get back, they'll be looking for this car.'

The Irishman pulled out a worn wallet and extracted some notes. 'It'd be cheaper keeping a yacht,' he said. 'Here's thirty and an end to the matter. Ask for your other one-fifty in London.'

'But will I get it?'

'You'll get it. And here's where you deliver, at eight precisely.' He opened a map of London.

The roads were greasy and the visibility came and went but Chas kept the Rover's wipers at work and made good time on the motorway. He reached London with time in hand. He idled away an hour in a cinema watching an erotic film without any great interest. He blamed his disinterest on his recent endeavours, turning his mind away from the fact that his habit was sapping his strength.

When he emerged, dusk and drizzle were falling together. He spent some more of The Irishman's money on a better meal than he could have afforded at home – dining out was expensive with a bird in tow. Emerging again into the bright lights, he recovered the Rover from a multi-storey car park and headed for the rendezvous as indicated by The Irishman's uncertain squiggles on the map.

At eight precisely he brought the car to a halt under a railway bridge beside the Thames Embankment and flashed his lights.

Six men came out of the shadows. Chas wound down his window. One of the men stooped to look in and passed an envelope. 'Hundred and fifty, right?' The Irish accent was barely perceptible.

Chas had provided himself with a pencil torch. He checked the money. It seemed to be all right. He had also moved the camera and binoculars to the back seat. 'The boot's not locked,' he said.

The man grunted. The group moved to the back of the car. The boot lid went up and he heard cases being removed. The leader re-appeared. 'We're a man short,' he said. 'Turned back at Liverpool. So we're leaving you one. Give it back to our friend.'

'Just a fucking minute.' Chas got out quickly and went

to the back of the car. One case had been left in the boot. 'Oh, no,' he said. 'Take this one and leave one of the others.'

Several of the men seemed to grin, including the leader, who said, 'We wouldn't do a thing like that. Not to a pal. And if we did, a bullet would be more than enough.' But he put his case back in the boot and took the other.

'Why not just put the gash one over the wall?' Chas asked. He nodded to where the Thames was sliding past, lights dancing greasily on its surface.

'That'd be a dead giveaway if it washed up. Do what you like with it, just as long as it's not found for a few days. So long!'

They melted into the shadows and were gone, but Chas thought that he could still feel eyes on him.

He thought that it was probably all right, but he was playing with the big boys. He drove round two corners, found a parking place outside a block of flats and got out, taking the camera and binoculars with him.

He walked back to the Embankment and continued until he found an all-night coffee stall. There he loitered the night away. Sloanes and their escorts stopped by, and pimps and prostitutes, all the capital's night people, most of them ready for a chat. He was propositioned by a homosexual and offered a job by a drunk who he thought was probably also a con man.

When dawn crawled reluctantly out of the chimneys in the industrial east, he walked back. The block of flats was still there. So also was the car.

He opened the boot. The case was unlocked. He lifted the lid – gently, although he could not have said what good gentleness could do. It was much as he had expected, but less complicated. There was a smell of putty coming from the explosive. The dry-cell batteries were already in place and connected to the timer although two leads hung free. The primer was embedded in the explosive, but the detonator was missing until he found it taped to the inside of the lid. There was also what he recognised, after a little thought, as a protective device, made very neatly from plastic. When the lid of the case was closed, a pair of metal contacts were held apart. When the case was opened, they would close. But at the moment a plastic strip fitted between them, attached to a string which could be led out through a small hole in the side of the case. When the detonator was placed, the lid closed and the string pulled, the case could not be opened without detonation – except, possibly, by somebody who knew exactly where the components were placed.

Chas left the car where it was but carried the case away with him. Apart from its intrinsic worth it must have a greater value in the right circles. Considerable sums could be extorted by the possessor of such a weapon. Not, Chas admitted to himself, that he would have the nerve to carry out a bomb threat; but he had at least one acquaintance who was less timorous.

He had intended to walk to the terminus and catch a train. But he was dog-tired. He did not have his supply with him, and Sunday public transport would not get him home until after his next fix was due. The sight of a new BMW parked out of public view tempted him and he gave way. It also had a full tank. There was even a fur coat, carelessly thrown on to the back seat. Chas decided that this might be his day.

To the average, clock-punching worker, Monday mornings are a limbo of numb frustration. Minds which have become attuned to leisure and metabolic clocks which have been allowed to run slow struggle to resume the disciplines of time and work.

Chas had never punched a clock, unless you were to

count the occasion when, under the combined influences of gin and marijuana, he had put his fist through the timepiece on a public house wall. Since his student days, he had rarely attempted to run to a timetable. Master of his own time, one day and hour was much the same as any other.

But this Monday morning was different. Chas knew the meaning of Monday-morningishness. He could feel Monday creaking in his joints, throbbing in his head and dripping from his nose. Monday was hell, especially a dank, autumn Monday without even the crisp expectancy of winter, or summer's fulfilment.

His troubles had started the previous afternoon. It had not been his day after all. He had sailed blithely along the motorway, singing to himself. He was happy. With a good mink to sell, he could have a long rest from the hazards and strain of larceny.

He treated himself to another good meal at a Services, entered the town by the back roads and abandoned the BMW on a double yellow line, two streets from home. The mink, the camera and the binoculars had been bundled in his own threadbare coat. He had left the bundle and the attaché case in a deserted wash house behind the flats while he scouted ahead, but Sylvia seemed to be out so he returned to fetch them.

He pulled out the bottom drawer of the chest of drawers. The space beneath was his only safe hiding place other than a small hole under the bathroom pipes where his drugs were cached. The attaché case, the camera and the binoculars fitted neatly into the space, but the mink had a mind of its own. However tightly he rolled it, the coat would rise up before he could put the drawer back. He gave up at last, replaced the drawer and he was standing with the coat in his hands, wondering where he could stow it, when Sylvia walked in on him.

'Fancy yourself in that, do you?' she asked.

Chas flushed. He had no alternative but to push it at her. 'I bought it for you,' he said. 'Celebrate my first earnings, like.'

Sylvia took the coat, turned it inside out and round about. She was no expert, but she came from a family where good coats were taken for granted. 'Pull the other one,' she said. 'On one day's driving? Oh, Chas, you haven't gone and bought something that's been nicked, have you?'

'Definitely not.'

Sylvia breathed again. She had closed her mind to the possibility that Chas might be crooked. 'How much did you pay?'

Chas wondered whether he could pass the coat off as dyed rabbit and decided that it was obviously too good. He made a guess at the lowest figure she would believe. 'Three hundred,' he said.

'What sort of shop sells a coat like this for three hundred nicker?'

'Pawnshop,' Chas said triumphantly.

'Oh.' Sylvia changed tacks again. 'Don't tell me that he paid you three hundred, just to drive him round London and back again? There must be something crooked going on.'

'No, of course not,' Chas said. 'But he's promised me steady work. I'm paying it off at ten a week.'

'You're out of your skull!' Sylvia exploded. 'Ten a week off your benefit! We couldn't live. And can you see me in mink?'

The argument had raged into the night, and when it ended their lovemaking had been a failure. Chas had become used to his own poor showing and put it down to trying too hard and too often; but this time was disaster. Sylvia had striven hard, but his recalcitrant flesh had never stirred.

Chas woke late, thick-headed and miserable. He was

sorely tempted to calm himself by advancing the time of his fix. But that, he knew, would be the first step towards the twice-a-day habit and a moribund sense of caution held him back. One thing he knew. Sylvia was going back to her parents soon, if he had to spend The Irishman's money on a taxi.

After breakfast of a sort – bread, marmalade and milkless tea – she had returned to the attack. 'Come on. Dress yourself. We're taking that coat back.'

'The pawnshop doesn't open today. Stays open weekends, closes Mondays.' Perhaps he could get away on his own and come to an arrangement with some amenable pawnshop proprietor.

'Well, all right, then. Tomorrow it goes back.' Sadly, she hung the lovely fur behind the curtain which served them for a wardrobe and came back to take his arm. 'Chas, it's not that I'm not grateful. You tried to do a nice thing. Stupid but nice. But it wouldn't be us. So I'll tell you what we'll do. We'll walk through the park to the town centre and we'll pick out something I'd like to have, nothing over ten quid at the most. And tomorrow, when we've got your money back, you can buy it for me and we'll pretend this never happened at all. I'll be surprised and very grateful for my lovely present. How about that?'

It sounded boring and boredom was Chas's great hate. He would far rather have gone back to bed and tried to sleep away his malaise. But the outing might give him the chance to slip away to a pawnshop. And, anyway, she might be a damned nuisance and she would have to go, but her eager eyes still had the power to move him.

'All right,' he said.

The park was empty and flowerless, a mess of dead leaves and newspapers blown together, but Sylvia loved to see the toy-like mandarin ducks on the pond. She threw them some dried crusts and talked to them.

They walked on and came to the main street of shops.

Idling along, they poked fun at the more outrageous fashions. Chas found that she could still make him laugh.

At a small antique shop, Sylvia admired a pendant in the window. Chas had his own reasons for avoiding that shop in her company, but they were not reasons which he could say aloud. He gave the proprietor a warning headshake over her shoulder and the man cut off a greeting.

The pendant was beyond their financial limit.

As the door closed behind them, Sylvia hesitated on the step. 'Wasn't that your friend The Irishman?' she said.

'Possibly,' Chas said. He had glimpsed a figure turning into a pub further along the road and on the other side. It had not looked quite like The Irishman, but it had been carrying an attaché case resembling the one which had been left in the garage. They moved next door and Chas stopped at the window of the electronics emporium. He liked to keep abreast of retail prices, so that he knew what to take and how much to ask. And he was curious. Even if it had been The Irishman, there could be no danger while he was still inside that pub.

'I don't want anything from here,' Sylvia said.

'I was looking at the prices of clock-radios, for later,' Chas said. 'I'll be needing an alarm when I'm in regular work.'

In spite of herself, Sylvia began to notice the electric toasters. The grill at the flat was broken.

Chas found himself looking at a large colour television which was telling its silent stories to the passers-by. The midday news was on. A street appeared and Chas thought that he recognised London. Beyond a reporter with microphone he could see police cars and ambulances, debris and a building without windows.

'You've seen them,' Sylvia said. 'Let's move on.'

'There's a ticket I can't read.' Chas focused on the

reflected image of the pub. The Irishman re-appeared without his case. He was wearing a pulled-down hat and there seemed to be the shadow of a moustache, but there was no mistaking the hollow chest and the bow-legged walk.

'It is him,' Sylvia said. 'I thought it was.'

'Don't look round!'

Chas spoke too late. Sylvia had turned. Diagonally across the street, The Irishman locked eyes with her. Then he turned his back and was walking away from them in short, jerky strides.

'He's forgotten his case,' Sylvia said. 'Shouldn't we tell him?'

Chas's mind seemed to have stalled in the middle of a nightmare. A few weeks before, a run of bad luck had resulted in a shortage of his necessary supplies. In the last hours before he could buy again from Fat Alec, he had seen strange animals coming out of solid surfaces. The experience had shocked him, but at least he had been able, by a great effort of will, to re-assure himself that these were figments of a rebelling nervous system and to separate in his conscious mind the hallucinations from reality. This was different. It was real and it was not going to go away.

He grabbed Sylvia's arm. 'We're going home.'

'But . . . '

'Don't argue. I'm ill. Flu, I think. I could collapse.'

She looked at him searchingly. 'You don't look well,' she admitted.

He hurried them back along their track, through the wrought-iron gates of the park, past the ducks and up the slopes of damp grass. He would have grumbled bitterly if she had set him such a pace, but she trotted to keep up with him.

Halfway home, she dragged him to a halt and pulled her arm free. 'He was planting a bomb, wasn't he?' she said. Her teeth were chattering.

He looked around. There was nobody in earshot, nobody watching them, nobody following. They might have been alone in the world and he wished that it could stay that way. 'I was afraid that he might be,' he said.

'He was wearing a moustache,' Sylvia said. 'He couldn't have grown one in the time. And he came out without the case he went in with.'

'You can't be sure it was the same man.'

'I'm sure. Chas, we've got to warn those people.'

'I'm not going back there.'

'Phone the police, then.'

'Not on your life.' Chas could envisage a thousand embarrassing questions which the police might ask. He gripped her wrist and, ignoring her protests, dragged her towards the haven of their home.

At the higher gate, already within sight of their flat she wrenched her arm away from him again and set off in her faintly ridiculous run in the opposite direction towards the bright paint of a phone box. Chas could have run after her. But what could he do or say, with people around? It was a relief, in a way, to have the decision taken out of his hands; but he viewed the future with sick apprehension.

Sylvia had almost reached the phone box when the deep concussion shook the town and put all the pigeons in the air.

She turned and walked slowly back towards him.

THREE

They had no television in the flat, for financial reasons although both affected to despise the medium. But their old radio picked up a station which was relaying news. The loudspeaker was strong with vowels but very weak on consonants so that they had to strain to understand. Even so, the urgency in the reporter's voice forced the news across.

A wave of six bombs planted in major London shops had been timed for 11 a.m. and five had caught the shoppers in droves. The sixth had been spotted by an alert store detective. The shop had been cleared in time to save everybody except the detective who, for some reason of his own, had stood guard over it. More than two hundred had been removed to hospital, many of them feared dead. Telephone lines had been made available for enquiries by next of kin. Damage was estimated at more than a million pounds. A phone call had claimed responsibility on behalf of the INLA, although no INLA or IRA spokesman had yet made an official statement. No arrests had been made so far and there was reason to believe that the bombers had been on a plane which had left Heathrow before the first bomb detonated.

News of the local bomb came in as late news. Lunchtime drinkers had been the target. A heavy toll had been taken but no figures were available. Again a phone number was given for anxious enquirers. The report finished by relaying a warning from Scotland Yard's Anti-terrorist Squad that everybody should be on the watch for abandoned cases and parcels – advice which in some areas would bring trade nearly to a standstill over the next few days.

Pop music took over.

Chas turned the volume down. 'Well, that's it,' he said.

Sylvia had collapsed into one of the disintegrating armchairs. 'All those people,' she whispered. 'And you wouldn't let me warn them.'

'You couldn't have got them out in time. And if we'd phoned we'd just have got a dozen coppers killed as well.'

'All the same . . . Chas, I've got to go to the police.'

'No.' All those questions . . .

'I can't just do nothing. Chas, how can I?'

'You do anything,' Chas said fiercely, 'anything at all, and if your name doesn't come out now it will when you have to give evidence.'

'That'll be months off,' Sylvia said. 'And he'd be inside.'

'There'll be an inquest,' Chas said. 'In the next few days. Remember who and what that man is. You think I want to sleep here, knowing that there might be a bomb against the door during the night?'

'I could go home.'

That would be worse. Sylvia at home and chattering could land him in a dozen different messes. 'You're the one he saw looking at him. If anyone in the pub noticed him, they're not likely to be talking. How long do you think it'd take him to find out where you live? I told him your name was Cantor. How many of those are there in the phone book? You want to bring this on your parents?'

She was quiet for a minute and he saw that she was shaking all over. At last she said, in a very small voice, 'Chas, what am I going to do?'

He was almost moved to pity, but that was an emotion

vhich he reserved for himself. 'Stay here for the noment,' he said. 'The Irishman knows you're my girl. Ie may be out looking for you. But he doesn't know vhere I live and he can't call attention to himself. It'll ake him at least the rest of the day to find this place. Vait here while I go and find somewhere safe to hide vhile we think about it.'

'All right,' she said. She pulled her knees up and urled into a ball, hugging herself for comfort.

Chas was glad to escape from the flat. Away from Sylvia's voice and those demanding eyes he had a chance of thinking. He dawdled slowly down through the park. ts emptiness was too total and he was glad when the lucks, associating the human figure with food, came bobbing his way. Silent companionship was what he needed. He hated to be alone or to be battered by voices. Ie wondered whether an association for the dumb could ntroduce him to a suitable bird. Appearance no object as long as she was guaranteed totally incapable of peech.

God, what a mess! Caught between The Irishman and he police and uncertain whether it would be better to be illed by the first or taken by the second and given the cold turkey cure. Sylvia was no longer a nuisance, she vas a walking trap. Without even meaning to shop him, he could spill a few words which would convict him of carrying the bombs to London. And if he went inside, it night not only be the cure. He could find himself sharing prison with men who had lost family to the bombs. Christ!

There had to be an answer.

If the silly bitch hadn't looked round, The Irishman vould never have recognised them from the back or, if he ad, would never have expected to have been recognised.

If.

He had to get out. But he must go with money in his pocket and an assured supply. He had most of The Irishman's two hundred, but that would last him less than a week. There were the binoculars and the camera, and the coat if he could get it away from her. But suppose that he went somewhere strange and could not make contact with a new source.

He needed something else to sell. A commodity. Could he mark up some heroin and sell it on?

A better idea hit him with such suddenness that, as he walked quickly off towards the town centre, his knees were shaking.

In the main street, dust had not finished settling over fire engines, police cars and the one remaining ambulance within the barriers. The front of the pub had gone and the neighbouring buildings, unslated by the blast, leaned into the gap. Windows for a hundred yards around were all agape. Rescue work was continuing in the dwindling hope of finding survivors, but hampered by an intrusive crowd, part curious, part indignant but mainly made up of anxious relatives. A woman's voice wailed something unintelligible.

Chas ignored the turmoil. It had no message for him. When he saw, in the gutter, a shoe containing the foot of an unfortunate who had been at the pub's door at the moment of the blast, he turned his face away. He only hoped that no part of himself ever lay around like that.

In the antique shop which they had visited earlier, the proprietor was moaning over a lovely Sheraton table, irreparably scored by flying glass. Several figurines which had stood on it, one of them Meissen, had been powdered. The door was jammed but the glass was out of the frame. Chas stepped through gingerly.

The dealer glared at him. 'Mind your feet, you could be walking on the last saleable item I've got. Oh, the crazy bastards! Look what they've done.' He was near tears.

Chas stepped carefully. 'Terrible,' he said, without caring. He was too full of his own woes.

'If you've come back for that pendant, it's flattened. If you've got something for me, it's not your time.'

'I've got something for you,' Chas said, 'but it's special and it won't wait.'

Nelson Daw gave him the appraising look which he might have aimed at a suspect painting and then nodded. 'Stand guard here for a few minutes while I phone for Jimmy to come and start clearing up. The phones around here are out and I didn't dare leave the place. Then we'll talk.'

Alone in the tumbled shop, Chas could have helped himself to a hundred unbreakable coins and snuffboxes. But who would have bought them from him?

As a young man, Nelson Daw had been a dilettante of the art world until financial pressure had forced him to commercialise his considerable knowledge. In the service of one of the premier antique dealers of the time he had earned a good wage, but he was soon discontented. There was money to be made in the trade, but not by wage slaves. When he spotted a miniature kitten carved out of nephrite by Fabergé among the odds and ends in a sale and bought the whole shoe box, which turned out also to contain a scarab, from under the noses of the other dealers and for less than a fiver, he was fool enough to do so in the firm's name. His employer pocketed the price of a new Rolls. Young Nelson was rewarded with a commission of twenty per cent on the purchase price.

He scraped together a little capital and opened his own shop, the same shop which, nearly thirty years later, had been devastated by The Irishman's bomb. But he had found himself little better off. His shop and his capital were not enough to furnish him with a competent assistant, and as a one-man band he could not be buying and selling at the same time. Then again, such finds as he did make were of benefit to the Inland Revenue almost as much as to himself.

It was only with the intention of increasing his capital and so making his business viable – although that usage of the word had not yet been coined – that he first traded in stolen goods. He meant it to be a short-term expedient. But it was so easy, so profitable and so tax-free, and his clients were so persuasive, that it had become a life's work. He had been an established fence for a quarter of a century; and never a conviction against him, although the ice had sometimes proved thin.

His trade in legitimate antiques was still his real love, but it could never have supported a life style which had grown ever more self-indulgent nor provided the retirement during which he planned to enjoy true luxury. His dream of a small but gracious mansion, furnished with perfect and perfectly matched antiques and staffed by a handful of perfect servants, was with him night and day. It would be the regular haunt of charming and famous people, and as regularly visited by beautiful prostitutes skilled in satisfying the older man's more outrageous whims. The huge total of necessary investments, in cash and kind, had been within sight for years, advancing with each coup or retreating with a business reverse or a surge of inflation. Another good year would be more than enough. Soon now, very soon.

In his neat and logical mind, his less legal activities divided themselves into three parts. A legitimate business would have called them departments or divisions and headed each with a director.

The quick turnover which he needed for immediate income and to finance his other deals was provided by a steady trickle of expensive goods which could, with care, be re-sold immediately on the open market. Anything was welcomed, from good wine to lace underwear, or from postage stamps to papers which could be used to legitimise a stolen, pedigree dog. But the mainstay was in the electronic goods. Chas had proved to be one of his best sources, together with another addict who specialised in car radios and tape players and a boatman from the docks fifty miles downriver who brought only yacht electronics – echo-sounders, radar, radio-navigation equipment, marine radios and auto-pilots. But other thieves, with less constant needs, knew where to come with their booty.

For these goods, a rhythm had been established over the years which was almost musical. Monday through Wednesday, for an hour before the shops opened and again after they closed, a van stood in the lane behind the shop. The lane was a dead end and its further side was the blank wall of a former cinema now devoted to bingo. The van was plain but was otherwise identical in make and colour to the two vans belonging to the electronics shop next door, so that even a surprise visitor to the lane – almost unknown at such hours – would have seen nothing to surprise him. The business had become so routine that, if Daw himself were away attending a sale, the van driver was authorised to pay cash, up to a quarter of the retail prices marked in the windows of the neighbouring shops. Often, the rubbish store behind the electronics shop provided also the appropriate boxes for the goods, or near enough not to matter. From Thursday morning, the van was away to the other side of the country where Daw had established, and the van driver maintained, contacts with a network of street and market traders.

Gold and jewellery, the second area of trade, were always profitable. But too little came his way. Disposal into the fringe of the legitimate market was too easy.

But it was in the purchase of art and antiques that Nelson Daw had made his real mark. Often, he was consulted before the robbery or even suggested the target in advance. These illicit treasures he bought (by appointment only and at remote rural meets) at prices gauged to the holding period which he judged necessary. Many minor pieces could be re-cycled quickly, although some of these might have to be smuggled abroad. The rest went into his secret store, to be disposed of when they had faded from memory. His computer-like brain held them all in a neat index. Some of the better-known pieces would not be saleable until they could buy him comfort in his old age. One Rembrandt could never be sold at all but might eventually hang in his private bedroom. And, mingled with the other goods, was a growing matched set of furniture, all conforming to Thomas Sheraton's cabinetmaker's book, with carpets and pictures and mirrors and even curtains, all destined for his future home.

These were his principal trading goods, but it was his boast that he would buy anything, provided only that it were moveable and that the price was right. He had a knack for finding a safe and profitable outlet for the most unlikely of goods.

But this proposition was something else again. As he listened to Chas, he scratched his bush of silver hair which had once been red-brown. He was still a handsome man in a heavy-jowled way, although his skin was puckered by old acne scars and too much good living was showing itself by way of broken veins. He was, as always, freshly shaven, manicured and dressed with a quiet excellence which went well with the elegant stock-in-trade.

They were sitting in his office, a cubicle overlooking the shop but cut out of the back shop where an elderly jack-of-all-trades came in when needed to re-furbish or repair. The office was tidy and functional but not by any standard luxurious. No customer ever saw inside it. Cheques were written on an escritoire in the shop.

For once in his career, Nelson Daw hesitated. It was not that he was shocked. One investment is much like another except that some are more durable than others. 'I don't know,' he said. 'I never bought a whole person before. I'm not a slaver.'

'You say you buy anything,' Chas said. 'And this time there's a ready market waiting.'

'A one-man market. If it doesn't come off, my investment's down the drain.'

'He's got to buy, whatever the price. Sylvia saw him go in and come out. She's almost certainly the only living witness and she's made up her mind to go to the police. Hell, I'd negotiate with him myself but I'm the one person who daren't go near him. He might decide that I'd be better out of the way as well.'

'He'd never have that sort of money.'

'Money,' Chas said scornfully. 'He wouldn't need it. You could make him open any safe in the country.'

That, Daw admitted to himself, was quite a point, but he went on probing for disadvantages. 'I might not be able to contact him,' he said. 'If he's any sense, he's gone to ground.'

'He hasn't any sense.'

Daw glanced through the panel of one-way glass to where the van driver was carefully separating salvageable antiques from fragments of glass and china and wood. 'That's true,' he said.

'And even if he has, he'll have to surface some time.'

'I wouldn't want to make this a long-term investment. Food costs money. And I couldn't keep her in the dark. If she lost her mind through sensory deprivation, she'd lose her value.'

'She doesn't eat much,' Chas said. 'Damn it, the word

is that you hid out the four bullion robbers for three months while you got rid of the gold for them.'

'Who the hell told you that?' Daw demanded.

'Just a rumour.'

'Don't you go repeating it. I'll tell you what I'll do. Deliver her to me and I'll cut you in for twenty per cent of my net profit.'

Chas shook his head violently and then had to wait for the nausea to pass. Regular drugging had played havoc with his inner ears. 'It must be cash,' he said. 'I must have a stake to get me away. I'll give you a better deal if you can get me some of it in horse.'

'Heroin, you mean?' This time, Nelson Daw was shocked. 'I've never dealt in that and never will. If you want to go on killing yourself you can do it on your own. Cash down, I could only go to a thousand. The police might get to him first.'

'It's not much for a life.'

'Now you listen to me,' Daw said severely. 'I don't care if it's a life or the Taj Mahal or a piece of moonrock. The only factors in my equation are what chance I have of getting how much and when. Working backwards, I come to one grand precisely. If that's not enough, peddle the goods elsewhere.'

'It'll have to do,' Chas grunted.

Daw nodded, which meant that a binding contract had been reached. 'Get her ready,' he said. 'Tell her that a nice gentleman is coming to take her to a safe place. I'll bring the van up myself in an hour or two. Jimmy'll have to stay and board up.'

'Bring extra money,' Chas said. 'I've got a fur and things.'

By now, Chas was convinced that The Irishman was only awaiting his chance to kill both Sylvia and himself. He was in a fever to lay in a stock of his drug in readiness for a total disappearance as soon as what he thought of as 'the other business' was completed.

Although he knew most of Fat Alec's favourite ports of call, he was hampered by the fact that these were scattered all over the city, by limited time and by the need to avoid being anywhere where he might meet The Irishman. What seemed an age spent dodging through alleys from bar to café to phone booth to bandstand to railway waiting room produced no sign of the pusher, and he was on the point of giving up the chase when he seemed to recognise a back which was disappearing down an underpass. He caught it at the far end and grabbed its elbow.

Humpey Waterboys, tall, thin and nervous, was one of the more brilliant post-graduate research students of his generation. He was also a fellow addict. His earnings alone would never have supported his addiction, but he was blessed or cursed with a very rich father who preferred to hand out a more than generous allowance rather than be plagued by a son who, quite unintentionally, made him feel like a dolt.

'Stop a minute, Humpey,' Chas panted. 'Rest those long legs. Want to ask you something.'

Humpey blinked at him for a few seconds. He had been deep in an abstruse problem in X-ray refraction and it took him a moment to identify himself before he could begin to wonder about the out-of-context person accosting him. 'Hullo,' he said carefully. 'Nice to see you again.'

'Listen,' Chas said. 'Are you seeing Fat Alec soon?'

That gave Humpey the clue he needed. He switched his mental scan from the student body to certain wild parties in a studio flat. The penny dropped. 'Why yes, Chas,' he said, as if the other's identity had never been in doubt. He looked at his bare wrist, frowned and dug a wrist watch out of his pocket. 'In about an hour.'

'Will you tell him . . . ' Chas paused. Humpey could forget a message. He could forget anything. 'Give him a note,' Chas said. He found a ballpoint pen in his pocket and fished a scrap of paper out of a refuse bin. 'A friend has about £500 to spend if the price is right,' he scribbled. 'Please leave word with barman in usual place where and when I can meet you. Chas.'

'You won't forget, will you?' he asked anxiously.

'Of course not,' Humpey said. He stuffed the note into a bulging pocket and walked off, thinking of X-rays again. He was wondering whether it would be worth writing a special computer program, just to produce a three-dimensional graph of his other results against varying wave-lengths.

Chas hurried home. He was late for his fix again and all his fears were curling above him like the memory of a wave which had nearly drowned him as a child. He also had the beginning of the shakes. But he divorced his mind from these unrealities. His problems might fade away. If Humpey remembered. If Fat Alec would deal. If Nelson Daw didn't get cold feet.

There was one if which Chas had forgotten. In his mind, Sylvia had become a goods parcel, without the right to a choice. But Sylvia had taken a different view. She had packed and gone.

FOUR

His first sensation was of relief. At least he did not have to shake her off while he fetched the electric kettle into the bathroom and went through the ritual of sterilisation. He prepared his syringe and put a tourniquet of a cord and a spoon round his upper arm to raise the veins. Within a few seconds the horrors were receding before the heavy dose. His head swam and then settled.

The start of the brief euphoria was blanked out by the realisation that her absence was not, after all, a blessing. With her had flown both his safety and the stake which he needed to carry him away from danger.

His brain was in top gear while the first kick of the drug lasted. He pieced together his recollection of their earlier talks while another part of his mind made plans.

When Nelson Daw stalled the van to a halt below the flat, he found Chas already waiting on the pavement with a bundle at his feet, shoulders hunched against a blustering wind.

'Open up the back,' Chas said. 'We'd better deal with this first.'

'Right.'

Secure in the back of the van among the stock already stowed, and amber-lit from the rooflight above, Daw grunted over Chas's offerings. The camera and binoculars were easily priced but the fur, while obviously good and readily marketable, was a matter of guesswork. He pitched it low. 'Eight hundred the lot,' he said.

Chas guessed that he was being ripped off, but he had no time for haggling. He decided to chalk it up as a favour to be reclaimed later. 'Cash as we go along,' he said.

Daw nodded. That was the rule of the game. 'Out you get,' he said.

'Don't forget the film.'

'I bet your Granny's an expert egg-sucker by now,' Daw said. The undeveloped film in a camera was the most damning identification. Moreover, it could repay the cost of developing. Private erotica were not unknown and if the subjects were identifiable there was a man in London who paid well for such wares. If they were unknown, there were other markets. A stockbroker from Guildford had been appalled to find that he figured, along with his secretary, in a bluer-than-blue magazine circulating among his colleagues.

Alone in the back of the van, Daw took a key from his pocket, rolled back a section of matting and unlocked a strongbox welded under the floor of the van. He counted off eight hundred pounds and transferred a thousand to an envelope in his pocket before locking and concealing the strongbox and climbing out.

Chas buttoned the eight hundred into the breast pocket of his khaki shirt. It gave him half of a bosom – a tit to suck during the weeks to come, he thought.

'Let's get into the front,' he said. 'The girl's run off.'

Daw climbed into the driver's seat. Chas sat beside him. Daw was frowning. Thinking it over, he had sold himself on the idea of having a skilled safe-blower entirely under his thumb. Retirement had begun to seem very close and very attractive.

'The deal's off, then?'

'Not necessarily,' Chas said. He was riding along on his high. 'Depends where she's gone. If she's headed for the fuzz she's probably home and dry by now and I'm on the run. But I rubbed her nose in the dangers of being a named witness. I think she's bolted for home, to drop the whole mess into Daddy's lap.'

'You reckon?'

'It's worth a twenty-mile drive, isn't it? We can still get there ahead of her, and I'll talk her into the van.'

Daw made up his mind. 'You drive,' he said. 'I'm one of nature's passengers.'

They changed places. Chas found his way through the unfamiliar gears and coaxed the heavy vehicle through the streets. Dark was near and patches of drizzle reduced visibility. Nelson Daw switched the lights on for him. They emerged on to a dual carriageway and bowled along through darkening countryside. The commuter traffic thinned out.

'Put her along,' Daw said.

'This is all she'll do without leaving the road,' Chas said through his teeth. The van, at speed, tended to swing with each gust of wind. 'If she caught a train, she'll have to change. The bus goes in and out of every village along the way. If she's thumbing for lifts, she may never get there at all.' A girl hitch-hiker had been murdered on that road not long before. 'And if she bumped into The Irishman, my problems are over.'

'Bully for you,' Daw said without enthusiasm.

They swung off the dual carriageway and took an A-road which found a way between low hills. When the wind punched through the valley it slowed the van until Chas had to change down. But soon a spattering of lights showed ahead. They ran between the street lamps again. Chas took several turnings, muttering to himself, made a wrong turn, retraced his way and picked up his direction from a posting towards another town.

They came out onto the road which ran between a stretch of common land and expensive private houses, set well back in large, picturesque gardens.

'That's it,' Chas said. 'The house with the half-timbering. I was at her birthday party once.'

Nelson Daw looked. There was a treble garage. He was suitably impressed although it was still not what he had planned for himself. 'There's no sign of excitement,' he said. 'I think we're here first.'

'I told you,' Chas said.

He turned the van in a driveway, drove past again and parked near the first junction in the puddle of darkness under some trees. 'Whichever way she comes, she'll have to pass here,' he said.

'If she takes a taxi, or phones her dad to pick her up, we've lost her.'

'She won't,' Chas said confidently. 'There was only a quid or two in the flat, and she's too bloody independent to want to be obligated. Especially to her parents.'

They waited. A shower plinked and plunked on the van's roof and passed on. Daw fetched a radio-cassette player from the stock in the back of the van and they had music of a sort.

'Have we guessed wrong?'

'Give it longer,' Chas said. 'She's a woman. No sense of time. Come to think of it, this could work out better. I'd rather she was seen heading for home than that she disappeared from the flat.'

Later, a small figure came plodding up from the bus terminus, rucksack on back and a cardboard box dangling from string-grooved fingers. Rain had returned and her hair was plastered to her neck. Chas waited until she was almost abreast of the van before he slid back the door and got out.

'Hello, Sylvia!'

She made as if to come towards him, and then to run away. Then she stood, swaying with tiredness, all spirit gone. 'You didn't come back and you didn't come back and I got scared,' she said. 'I made up my mind to visit home. Daddy can take me somewhere safe and The Irishman need never know I've been here.'

Chas's high was already past. He would be no more than his debilitated self until withdrawal began next morning. He had to struggle to find logic.

'He's there before you,' he said. 'We went past your house. He's in a car outside.'

'Then if I go to the police, they can catch him and it's all over?'

'But suppose they miss him, or let him out on bail. He'll know that you've shopped him. He could bomb your house just for revenge. He's that sort.'

She was too dispirited to see the flaws in his argument. Her look of hope melted away. 'There must be something I can do,' she said.

'Leave it to me,' Chas said. 'Go with this gentleman. You've met him before. He has a safe place where you can stay and nobody can get at you.'

She swayed forward and leaned against his chest for a moment. 'All right,' she said. She reached up and kissed his cheek. 'Please, don't take any more of that stuff. For my sake. It's changing you.' Then she turned away and lifted her box into the van.

Nelson Daw moved across to make room for her. Chas walked round the back of the van. Daw's arm was hanging casually from the driver's window. Chas took the envelope out of his fingers. As he walked away he heard the van's engine start.

He never looked round.

With money in his pockets, Chas treated himself to the luxury of not stealing a car. He went back by train. The barman in The Stately Arms, who acted as Fat Alec's postbox, had a note for him.

Nelson Daw's secret warehouse was a legend among criminals, many of whom would have sold their sisters for a chance to empty it. As with all legends, its very existence was asserted by some, denied by others. Its secrecy remained inviolate.

The Tyburn Sanitaryware factory was a huge building on a 150-acre site. Daw owned a small part of it. At one time, briefly, he had owned it all.

Fifteen years earlier, Daw had been approached by a group of property speculators of the smaller and shadier sort. They knew him as a man who would sometimes raise money for a share in a venture if the odds looked good. One of their number had discovered that the firm of Tyburnware had received an offer for their factory in Westonburn, which they had already outgrown, from a giant neighbour in similar difficulties. The offer had been too good to refuse. The Tyburnware directors were searching with increasing desperation for replacement premises. It would be only a matter of time before they learned that a certain pottery was in the hands of the receiver. There was skilled labour on the dole and the local clay was excellent.

Daw had gone to look for himself and what he had seen had given him to think furiously. The problem of storage had been exercising his mind. Renting lofts and barns and lockups was dangerous. Police and thieves had both found his caches on occasions.

The pottery was virtually in open country although it had its own townlet for support. It was fronted by tidy lawns which lay along a rural B-road. The visitor rounded the building on its left and found loading bays and car parks extending to where the boundary fence, in line with the far end of the building, marked the edge of a thick wood. For no evident reason, only a rough track led down on the right of the building to where a quite superfluous basement door existed, just short of the same woodland.

Daw had raised the money on his own account, cutting out his would-be partners and buying the land and building for himself. Three weeks later he had sold it again. After all costs were met he had shown a small profit. Even if he had made a loss he would have been satisfied, because during his short ownership there had been built a brick wall which sealed off the last forty feet of basement.

It is doubtful whether any surviving members of the Tyburnware staff realised that their basement was shorter than the rest of the building. The deeds were held by Daw himself and by the lawyers of the parent firm in Zurich. The basement was only used for the storage of patterns and moulds of sanitary fittings long obsolete. If the Grand Hotel suffered breakage of one of the twenty or so huge, original, willow-pattern washbasins, they could replace it at a cost which might be heavy but would probably be less than the cost of replacing the other nineteen and re-tiling the whole of the gents. At such times, a search was made of the basement. Otherwise, it was unentered.

Where the extra door had once confronted the explorer there was now a secure but carefully ramshackle garage for Daw's van. Even if some aspiring thief or detective had managed to follow the van there, he would have found only the van's overnight shelter.

Nelson Daw hauled the van round into the mouth of the track, bounced through potholes which his driver would have avoided from long practice and found the garage doors rushing into his lights. He slammed on the brakes and skidded to a halt in time. When he stopped the engine, the headlights died and the sidelights painted a gentler glow over the patchwork frontage. The van sighed with relief.

'Thank God!' Sylvia said. 'I was beginning to think I'd be safer with The Irishman.' Her spirits had recovered some of their usual resilience during the drive.

Daw smiled absently. He was watching the mirror, but

as usual there was no sign of a follower. Surreptitiously, his hand went behind the seat. 'The Irishman's the one person you'd be in greater danger with, and don't you forget it,' he said. 'What did you really see this morning? Anything?'

Sylvia closed her eyes and remembered. 'I saw a man go into the pub across the street and along a bit from the antique shop. He was carrying an attaché case. Even from the back I recognised The Irishman and I said so to Chas. He came out a few minutes later without the case and although he was wearing a pulled-down hat and what I suppose was a false moustache I knew him for sure. And he knew me, I could tell that when our eyes met.'

'And you're prepared to give evidence?'

'Like a shot.'

'I just wanted to be sure,' Daw said. He pulled out a ring of keys. 'Come along, now. It isn't The Ritz. You'll have to rough it tonight, but my driver will bring you some comforts in the morning.'

Like the gentleman which he had been and hoped to be again, he carried her rucksack for her into the garage. When the doors were closed, he switched on a light. Double doors in the factory side of the garage looked as though they had been nailed into place only to fill a gap, but he swung them aside. Behind were substantial oak doors which he unlocked. A brick recess finished at yet another door, this time of bars. Daw fumbled with his keys and then felt for a light switch. A pattern of bare bulbs came alive showing a cavern of brick walls and concrete floor and ceiling.

Much of the floorspace was taken up with neat stacks neatly covered with dust sheets, but in the far right-hand corner there was a space, screened by the stacks, in which four camp beds stood in a tidy row. On one bed was a pile of blankets which seemed to be reasonably clean. In the corner was a tap over a floor drain, a broom, a kettle, a plastic basin, a small, single burner camping stove and a roll of lavatory paper.

'You were right,' she said in a small voice, 'it isn't The Ritz.'

'Jimmy'll bring you food in the morning. You won't be cold, there are kilns just above you. Be good.'

'Don't lock me in,' she said.

He slammed the barred door. 'There's some valuable stuff in there,' he said. 'And you'll be safer this way.' He closed the oak doors. She heard him turn the key. The doors fitted well. She listened but she could hear no more over the insidious muttering which she supposed came from the kilns.

She could not reach the light bulbs to take them out. The scale of the basement disturbed her. With the broom handle she broke the bulbs, sweeping up the glass fragments as she went, until only the living corner was illuminated.

She put on the kettle and then unpacked her possessions onto one camp bed and spread blankets on another. When the water was hot, she stripped off her damp clothes, filled the basin and gave herself a meticulous flannel bath. She had only a small hand towel but she managed to dry herself. She felt better, so she filled the basin again and washed her hair, using the last of her shampoo.

For a loo, she had to squat, Arab-fashion, over the floor drain and then run the tap.

By the time when she could think of nothing more to do, she felt more able to face up to her other thoughts. Leaving the single bulb alight rather than grope the length of the cellar in the dark, she got between the blankets. She would have liked to have curled into a ball, but instead she stretched on her back and hung her hair over the end of the campbed to dry. She thought of Chas and of her family. She wondered whether anyone, anywhere, was thinking of her. Except, of course, The Irishman.

She fell asleep at last.

When she awoke, muzzy-headed, it might have been after ten minutes or ten days. The kilns were still murmuring overhead, the surviving bulb spilled its harsh light and the cellar was mildly warm. Her watch was never really reliable but it was still running and it said that the time was after eight – in the morning, she presumed. She remembered to wind it up. The watch was her only measure of time.

She drank some water and performed her ablutions all over again. She was already cleaner than she had ever been during her time with Chas, but it seemed important. She tried to find something in her meagre wardrobe to boost her morale, but her clothes had been chosen for conformation to a type and here, where there was no crowd with which to merge, she found them repellent.

There was a sound at the door and a glow of daylight spread across the ceiling. A soft voice called, 'Are you there?'

'Of course I'm here. Where else could I be?' she called back and then, in sudden fear that he might take offence and leave, she added, 'Wait a minute. I'm just getting dressed.' Eager for any sort of companionship, she made a quick selection, dressed and hurried along one of the alleys to the barred gate.

A thin youth – he was about her own age but seemed younger – was kneeling outside the gate. He had unpacked a carton of groceries, forced the box through the bars and was patiently re-packing it on her side.

'Wouldn't it be easier to open the door?' Sylvia asked.

He looked up and blushed. 'Mr Daw didn't give me the key.'

Sylvia's vague anxieties had lifted with rest and company and she was in a mood for banter. 'Is he protecting me from you or you from me?' she asked. 'Which of us does he think is going to leap on the other?'

He seemed to blush easily. This time his original blush turned scarlet. He shook his head.

'Come on,' Sylvia said. 'You can tell me. Are you a known rapist or something?'

'He said he didn't want to put temptation in my way,' the boy muttered. 'But he was only joking.'

'That was very considerate of him.' She felt an irresistible urge to keep teasing. 'I feel much safer. What goodies have you brought me? Just food?'

'And a plate and things.'

'I bet you forgot a tin opener.'

'I didn't, then.'

'Well done. But there's no pans and things here. Just a kettle.'

Still kneeling, he looked up at her. 'I didn't know that,' he said sadly. 'Look, give me a list of what you need and I'll bring it tomorrow. Don't miss anything off, mind, because after tomorrow I'll be away for the rest of the week.'

'I hope I'll be out of here by then,' Sylvia said and then realised that the hope was rather thin. If The Irishman had been caught, there would have been no need for the supplies. 'But, thanks. Just in case I'm not. I haven't any money, though. I could give you a cheque. My allowance ought to be in the bank by the time you get back from your travels.'

'Doesn't matter. Pay me when you get home.' He stood up in one lithe movement. 'I'll get a pen and paper out of the van.'

He left a succession of doors open and Sylvia found that she could see a slice of the outside world, fretted branches against a blue sky. It was provoking that the sun should be shining now after a week of cold and damp. A small bird was flitting around, not appreciating its freedom in the least. She was the one in the cage.

Jimmy came back from the van with a pad and a ballpoint pen and handed them through the bars. Sylvia poised the pen. 'Would a radio be too much to ask?'

'I can get that now.' He went back to the van.

Sylvia started her list. Books. Clothes. Washing powder. Saucepans.

Jimmy came back with the radio-cassette which Nelson Daw had used the night before. 'I could give you a telly,' he said, 'except that we haven't got a slimline to go between these bars.'

'Never mind about a telly.' Sylvia added to her list. Cassettes (classical). Spare batteries. Shampoo. The list seemed to go on and on. When she had finished, she held it up for him to see. 'If you can't manage it all,' she said, 'it doesn't matter. It seems an awful lot.'

He ran his eye down the list. 'What books?'

'Almost anything. Not too rubbishy and not too heavy.'

'Put down your favourite writers.'

When she came to think about it she found that her taste was dated. At university she had read almost nothing but her textbooks. And Chas, no great reader himself, had not encouraged reading. But it might be comforting to browse among the favourite authors of her teens. Once she started, she filled another page.

She held the list up again. He frowned at it. 'What clothes?' he asked.

'Anything,' she said. 'I haven't a decent stitch and nothing to change with.'

'Make a list,' he said. 'I don't know what girls wear.' And it would be exciting to see it written in her own hand. 'Put your sizes.'

'Stand up against the bars,' she said. She stood facing

him, their noses almost touching. 'We're much of a size,' she said, keeping a straight face. 'What fits you will fit me. Try them on in the shop. I dare you.'

This time his blush surpassed anything which had gone before. He backed away. 'Not on your nelly!' he said. 'Write your sizes and I'll see what I can do. No promises.'

When the list was complete, he was ready to go.

'Let me look out a little longer,' she said.

But there was a limit to how long you could enjoy looking at bare branches and one damn bird. When he said, 'Look, I'll have to go or I'll never get your list done,' she turned away and picked up the carton of foodstuffs.

'Get me some spare light bulbs,' she said over her shoulder. 'If that one pops, I'm in the dark.'

'Righto.' The door shut and she was back with her solitude.

She was hungry. She managed to boil an egg in the kettle and to get it out with a spoon and a fork before it was altogether solid. Then she had to wait for it to cool down before she could eat it. She had forgotten to put an egg-cup on the list. The business of breakfast and washing up passed another hour. And it was easier with the radio for company, voices and music and a sense of passing time. She tried to imagine the shy boy buying her underclothes and found that she was laughing.

FIVE

The Irishman seemed to have vanished off the face of the earth. That, at least, was his intention. His solo gesture on the day of the bombs had been rash, although he justified it to himself as a gallant action. But the recognition which he had seen on Sylvia's face had shaken him. The Anti-terrorist Squad would be working flat out to find the bombers, and by calling attention to his own town he had made sure that they would be doing the rounds of it, brandishing Identikit portraits of every known bomber and enquiring about Irish accents and sympathies. A quick departure and a cautious return seemed to be indicated.

Nelson Daw was unconcerned. He would have been worried if the subject of his investment had hung around, inviting arrest. The Irishman would be back.

Although The Irishman's safe-breakings were aimed at ready cash, he did not turn aside if jewellery should turn up in the same safe. Even the family silver, hammered flat (he was not one to be mean with his explosives) had its value. The Irishman had been an occasional visitor at the shop.

Nelson Daw liked to know who he was dealing with. Knowledge of the other's strengths and weaknesses could help him to a better bargain or to avoid dangerous mistakes. He had not even needed to leave his desk. The purchase of some rare coins (which The Irishman had found in a private safe along with some banknotes which would have interested the Inland Revenue) had been consummated in a half-bottle of Irish whiskey, quite enough to undo that already loose tongue.

The Irishman had a lady-friend, a plump ex-barmaid who had already borne him a child. Rather than risk her involvement if he should be caught, he had installed her in the adjacent flat and made sure that the landing was empty each time he crossed it. They were never seen out together, but Daw was in no doubt that The Irishman had given her whatever he had in place of a heart. Why the terrorist should have fallen for one billowing lump of female flesh among millions Daw could not make out, and The Irishman in his cups was far from coherent on the subject. Perhaps it was only that, for the first time ever, somebody loved the stunted, vicious little man in return. Whatever the reason, he would not be away for long.

Daw found time to visit the lady, first making sure that she was not yet under any observation. She had clearly been warned to speak to nobody, but she could hardly refuse entry to a gentleman who so eloquently admired her only three interests in life – her baby, her spotless (if fussy) flat and her darling Sean. Daw was too cautious to leave a letter which might be found if the police got too close on The Irishman's heels, but he impressed on her, more than once, that it was essential for her lover's safety, future prosperity and chances of avoiding eternal damnation that he visit the antique shop the very minute of his return to the town.

Daw might have worried more about his investment, but his days had suddenly become very full. Months before, a small manor had come on the market. It was two hundred miles away but he went to visit it and found that it was very close to his ideal. Through two firms of solicitors (one of them abroad) he had opened negotiations. He had not expected a successful outcome – it was, he thought, the sort of deal in which the executors feel obliged to advertise while having a purchaser already on the hook. But, on reaching home after depositing Sylvia with the rest of his stock-in-trade, he had found a letter advising him that his offer had been accepted.

His alternative identity had been established long before and carefully fostered over the years. But, in the rush of arranging to sign a contract as his other self, bringing back money from a multitude of foreign bank accounts and beginning to dispose of the liquid assets of which Sylvia was only a comparatively minor item, he had no time to think about The Irishman whom he had labelled 'Pending' and filed away in his tidy mind.

The girl was on ice. She would keep.

Jimmy Noble had worked for Nelson Daw for nearly three years.

It happened that the previous driver, although he exuded a great air of respectability which made him an asset to Daw's business, was easily tempted into other illegalities and, having overnight access to the van, was considered to be equally an asset by his associates. This had been quite unknown to his employer.

One night, the group had gone after lead from a church roof. Their activities had gone unnoticed all night and they had continued stacking the flattened sheets in the vehicle long after common sense should have told them that the van's volume could hold a far greater weight of lead than it had ever been designed to carry. At dawn, when the first traffic warned them that it was time to be moving off, the van was sitting hard down on its stops. The men had piled into the front, exchanging jubilant speculations as to the value of their haul. Being parked on a downhill slope, the van had moved off in almost its usual style. They had a straight run long enough to build up speed and only at the first roundabout had the driver discovered that the van was impossible to brake or to steer. It had brushed a

Daimler contemptuously out of its path, crossed the central reserve and the further roadway and pulped its occupants against the concrete abutment of a bridge.

Daw had emerged without stain. His insurers had even furnished the money for another van. But the incident which had been lethal to his driver had been dangerous, in a different way, to Nelson Daw.

He became his own driver again, and business suffered accordingly, while he worried about finding a suitable replacement. It seemed impossible to find a totally trustworthy man to handle stolen goods. It was another example of what Sylvia had called a contradiction in terms.

Within two months, instead of finding Jimmy, Jimmy had found him.

The new van had developed a fault while in its dilapidated garage and refused to start. The local garage, where he had bought it, had recently gone out of business and was up for sale, so that no expert help was available nearby. Daw was vainly trying to start it with jump leads, at the risk of flattening the battery of his Rover, when a soft voice behind him said, 'Trouble?'

Daw glanced first to reassure himself that his store was concealed and then looked up. The late-teenager had been in evidence around the now-defunct garage – the son, it turned out, of the liquidated proprietor.

In silence, the stripling had taken over his tools and within a few minutes had found and rectified the fault, then cleaned contacts and filters and tuned the engine. Daw was impressed – the van felt better than new. He soon learned that the boy was intelligent and a good driver. He was also a very silent person.

Jimmy was tested with a few deliveries which were perfectly legitimate but which he was allowed to believe were shady. The deliveries were made without a word getting out. Next he was sent with an unlocked box which, Daw stressed, must not be opened. It arrived at Daw's friend with the secret seal intact.

Jimmy was soon doing the long run on his own.

He liked working for Mr Daw. The hours might be long but the money was plentiful. He met people without being forced to converse; on that side of the law, his reticence was counted in his favour. He had no desire to work among colleagues who might make demands on him. His only regret was that his job gave him no easy introductions to girls. One or two early refusals had made him shy at the flirtation game.

Shopping on behalf of a girl had been a new experience and a thrill. It had made him feel gallant and he had spread himself. Being both a private and a thrifty person, his substantial salary and commission had been accumulating in his Giro account. Lavishing it on Sylvia had hardly made a dent.

Without making more than a cursory examination of the shopping, Sylvia was stunned. Even her glimpse of the outside world took second place. Thirty paperbacks, several carrier bags printed with a variety of clothes shop names and whole cartons of miscellaneous necessities, even luxuries. He seemed to have ransacked the music shops for cassettes.

'Crikey!' Sylvia said. 'I can't pay you for this lot. I can give you a cheque for fifty dated next week. I'll have to owe you the rest.'

'Doesn't matter,' he said gruffly.

She wondered whether he was expecting a kiss, or more, for his kindness, but decided to leave him to ask for it. 'Is there any news?' she asked. 'About when I'm getting out of here?'

He shrugged. Mr Daw never told him anything except what to do.

'It's been good of you anyway,' she said. 'I'll gloat over it all when you've gone. I suppose you have to rush f again?'

'I'm free today. If you wanted company . . . '

'I do. And I'd like to go on seeing out.'

There was an awkward silence. They seemed to have aid it all. So much, Sylvia thought, for his company. She tched the radio-cassette and put on one of the new pes. Puccini. He seemed to like it.

'You play chess?' he asked suddenly.

'Yes, I do. Do you?'

'I'll go and get my board.'

'Lovely!' she said. 'I'll change into something clean efore you get back.'

'No,' he said quickly, and this time his flush was candescent.

She was puzzled for a moment and then she underood. 'You want to . . . be here when I dress?'

He nodded dumbly.

In the past, she had stripped and more for lesser ndnesses. But instinct told her that he was not after an otic display. He would prefer a stolen glimpse of aidenly innocence. 'We haven't known each other very ng,' she said.

He shook his head.

'We'll have to think about it,' she said. 'You go and get our chessboard. Can you leave the doors open?'

Again the headshake. 'Mr Daw's orders.' That seemed settle the matter.

While he was away, she carried her new possessions nder the light and laid them out. They took up another mp bed. There seemed to be food for a fortnight, ostly tinned but much of it expensive luxuries.

His choice of clothes – and how she wished that she ould have seen him in the shops! – revealed a not ncommon ambivalence. Association with Mr Daw and ith the artifacts of the past had taught Jimmy taste, in ne and colour if not in fashion. The two cotton dresses

suited her mood, simple and young, almost schoolgirlis
The underwear was from a different shop. It was of
style which assumed that it would not always be hidden.

He had remembered paper tissues, which she ha
forgotten.

He was back quickly and she guessed that his hom
was not far away. When he saw that she was still in he
jeans and T-shirt he smiled shyly and then looked awa
Fumbling in embarrassment and not meeting her eye, h
put up a small card table against the bars and laid out
cheap chess set.

She made up her mind. 'Wait there,' she said.

She went back to the living space, where she was out
his sight, and changed into new bra and pants. The br
was slightly generous and she padded it with pape
handkerchiefs. She felt silly in frills and lace which ha
never been her style. She moved, as if unwittingly, to
position where he could see her along the length of one
the alleyways and in semi-darkness. As demurely as sh
could, she put on a slip and one of the cotton frocks. Sh
brushed her hair out and tied it with a ribbon from one
the boxes.

Jimmy went outside. He was gone for several minute
She thought that she knew what he was doing. In a wa
it was a compliment. He came back with two foldin
garden chairs and slid one through the bars, fumbling t
extend it for her.

It was too cool for comfort with all the doors open b
at least she had her awareness of the outside world. The
spent a peaceful day playing chess while music lappe
around them. He was an adequate player, she wa
slightly better. Whenever she paused to think about h
move, Jimmy would make a nervous trip to the doors t
ensure that no stranger was approaching down the trac
She made lunch for them both.

At four, he said that he had to go.

‘So I’m on my own until . . . when?’

‘I’ll try to be back Sat’day night.’

‘And that’s it? Mr Daw won’t be coming?’

‘Shouldn’t think so. He’s busy. But you got your things now,’ he said. ‘You’ll manage. ’Course you will.’

‘Yes, of course I will,’ she said as cheerfully as she could. ‘Thanks to you.’

He gathered up his furniture, muttered something inarticulate and left. In retrospect, she thought that she had heard him say that she was beautiful.

SIX

The Irishman had gone north.

In this age of mobility all cities are near everywhere else, but at the time when emigration from Ireland was at its peak the emigrant's first stop was in Glasgow or Liverpool and many settled in one or other of those cities. Among the Glasgow-Irish, his accent would be unnoticed and his identity safe.

He was low on funds but a cousin had offered him a bed and a job with his small plumbing firm. He was as good a plumber as he was an electrician. For a few days he repaired burst pipes and overhauled boilers. At the end of the week, the two men, as a matter of course, went out to get drunk.

The Irishman – our Irishman – was by far the drunker of the two. He awoke with all the devils of hell clawing at his insides and his cousin's voice pounding at his brain.

'You're a damned fool, Wilf, you always were and I see no sign of you getting any wiser.'

With some difficulty he raised enough spittle to moisten his mouth. 'Don't call me Wilf,' he said. 'What've I done now?'

'How much do you remember?'

'I remember up to the Queen's Bar and the barmaid with the lopsided tits.'

'So you told her. I'll never show my face in there again. It was after that you started talking about . . . other things.'

The Irishman managed to feel even worse. 'The Cause?'

'Sure, on its own that wouldn't have mattered. The most of them agreed with you. But you went on to talk about the bombs.'

'Dear God! Tell me that I didn't say I made them!' He had been letting his beard grow. The pale stubble had hardly shown; but now, against his deathly pallor, it stood out like mould on a peach.

'Not in so many words,' said his cousin. 'But if any one of them was in doubt that you knew more than you were saying, he was drunker than you were and so he's probably dead by now. I doubt if it'll be long before one of them wants to buy a favour from the police and tells them about it.'

He swung his legs over the side of the bed and found that he was still dressed. It struck him for the first time that the room was strange. 'Where are we?'

'Where doesn't matter. I couldn't take you home. It would only have taken one of your last night's audience to be found trying to drive a car and the police would have been looking for you within minutes.'

A door opened. An enormous woman wearing only a half-slip walked through the room and disappeared through another door. She simpered at The Irishman as she went by.

'Holy Jesus!' he said. 'I never saw the like of that since I was weaned. I'd best be getting out of here. Do you have any money?'

'I did have,' his cousin said, 'but we drank it last night. I'll go out now and see if there's a fool will lend me some more. While I'm gone, Agnes will dye your hair and your beard. Where'll you go? London?'

'Not London. I was warned that if I set foot in the Smoke I'm dead. I'll see if Uncle Bob can have me in Liverpool.'

'And I never saw you in my life before you turned up at the beginning of the week.'

The Irishman's brain was beginning to work again. 'You can do better than that,' he said. 'Tell them you're sure I'm the bomber. Help them with an Identikit but don't make it too good. And say that I let slip I was going to Dundee to meet some sympathisers. That should draw them off. Then maybe I can sneak home for a bit. My loins are telling me it's a long time since I saw my girl.'

Sylvia was totally alone for three days and nights.

At first she was contented. She had books and music, leisure, safety, privacy, even comfort of a sort, everything which she would once have counted as the essentials for happiness.

But, on the second day, the monotony made her restless again. She decided that eternal sunshine, or a perfect but unchanging diet, even bacon and eggs, would pall. And the traditional concept of heaven would be so boring that, surely, they must have muddled it with hell.

She did a quite unnecessary laundry, hanging it to dry with some string which Jimmy had provided. And then she prowled restlessly among the covered stacks. She wondered whether she could hang some of the dust sheets to demark her own space and to exclude the pale mountains which loomed at her. She pulled down one of the covers and realised that she had no need to make do with camp beds for furniture. Here, among the packing cases and marquetry boxes, were carpets and furniture to satisfy a queen.

She moved the camp beds into one of the aisles and, after a struggle which left her breathless, dragged out a carpet which seemed to be of suitable size. It was going to be dusty work so she changed into her old jeans. She rolled out the carpet. It was a Chinese carpet, royal blue with the Romanoff eagle motif in each corner and the deepest, softest pile which she had ever imagined.

The carpet was so perfect that she could hardly bear to

put one of the camp beds on it, but the only other bed which she could find was a four-poster and much too heavy for her to move on her own, as were the several wardrobes. She found instead a Queen Anne chest of three long and two short drawers, a serpentine front and fishtail ends which, with the drawers removed, she managed to shift. She fetched the drawers and stowed her possessions neatly away.

The only tables which she could both reach and handle were a pair of sofa tables from around 1805, veneered in zebrawood with gilt brass stringing. She placed them carefully under the overhead light. The matching chairs were lost somewhere in the stacks so she chose instead a set of giltwood fauteuils – signed by Hertaut and upholstered in Beauvais tapestry, had she but noticed – and arranged four of them round the tables. One would have been enough for her needs but it would have emphasised her solitude.

The light was harsh. If there were any lampshades they must be in the packing cases which were solidly nailed up. She improvised a shade, rather cleverly, she thought, from one of the cartons and an old vest, and climbed on to the table to fix it.

She appropriated two standing mirrors and placed them where they would suggest doorways into other rooms of similar opulence.

It began to look good, so good that the barred gate might have been defensive rather than imprisoning. The furniture was ornate – inevitably, because, apart from that intended for Nelson Daw's retirement home, the store was used for pieces so distinctive that they would be identified from their descriptions in sale catalogues until memories had faded. There was no way to lessen the contrast between the island of luxury and the brick and concrete ocean so she decided to enhance it.

She went in search of ornaments. She climbed a stack

of furniture and replaced one of the light bulbs. The renewed glow led her to a stack of boxes. She opened several of them. Most contained ornaments representing subjects of sentimentality, shepherdesses and the like, but in a teakwood box she found a jade figure of Chow Kok Koh. The Chinese philosophy behind the symbolic figure was unknown to her, but the exquisite carving and the fact that he was sitting backwards on his mule so that, like herself, he knew where he had been but not where he was going, appealed to her. She moved it to the tables.

Probing into what had been the darkest corner, she came across the pictures, slotted into a purpose-made rack. She was not sure that she could manage to hang pictures, but she looked through them anyway, pulling them out one at a time.

Her first impression was that they were all, in different ways, works of brilliance. Line and colour, texture and light, were manipulated with uncanny skill. And these were not reproductions, they were real canvas and real paint, real genius and real signatures. As she worked her way along the rack, savouring, she realised that she had seen more than one of them in books or calendars. She stopped and went back two frames to a scene by Turner. Real light from a burning skyscape spilled over a dramatic composition of docks and cranes. She had seen it before, in monochrome but unmistakably. It had accompanied a newspaper article about a robbery. Lord Sefley's country seat had been entered and priceless furniture taken along with pictures and gold and silver. The Sefley coat of arms had also been illustrated and although she could not remember its details she thought that it had resembled the arms on the four-poster.

She could manage without pictures. She climbed up and removed the light bulb, burning her fingers through a handkerchief, and then set about re-covering the stacks as neatly as she could.

Her hands were black and she was sweating after what had been hard work. She treated herself to another sponge-bath and washed out her slacks and sweater. Then, back in one of her cotton frocks, she lay down on her camp bed and resumed her reading, looking up occasionally to draw comfort from her new setting. It was difficult to concentrate. Once or twice she found herself sucking her thumb, a habit which she had broken years before but which sometimes returned in times of stress.

While Sylvia was managing no more than to survive and was escaping from the horrors into her books and music, Chas was as close to happiness as he had been for as long as he cared to remember.

Aiming for wherever The Irishman was least likely to be, he took the train to a seaside resort, pampering himself with a first-class ticket in recompense for the squalid life which he had been leading and which was now, he hoped, gone for ever. He found an inexpensive hotel with rates further reduced because of the season, and took a room on the ground floor of an annexe. The ability to enter or leave without passing the desk had sometimes proved useful in the past.

For a few days he was content to stroll around the town, enjoying a coffee here and a modest drink there, relishing the peace and the bright autumn sunshine. Relieved from the need to break into an average of a house a day – more if the occupants of the first house had not moved with the times – he felt relaxation softening the knots inside him. Some of Nelson Daw's money had been spent on new clothes of careful casualness. He could have been mistaken for an off-duty golf pro.

Inevitably, boredom set in. His threshold of boredom had always been low and he was used to activity and to having obstacles in his way as challenging as mountains to be climbed. He could have relieved his life by increasing his daily dose. It would have been the next, logical step in his path. He fought it off, more to postpone the need to renew his supply than out of respect for his system. Instead he decided to seek out what bright lights were still lit in those parts.

There was a disco in one of the plushier hotels. He treated himself to a couple of gins and joined the small throng of dancers. Many were locals and seemed to know each other. This was as much an advantage as a snag. The girls were looking for new blood, men who had not let them down in the past.

Towards midnight, he was beginning to wonder which bird he had the best chance of pulling that night.

A similar topic was being discussed at a corner table between a blonde girl and a muscular man in tweeds. The girl could have passed for twenty, but she was in her thirties. Nature had given her the features of a baby, and art still managed to keep her skin and flesh in harmony with her baby face.

'I don't know why we bother,' she said. 'There's hardly a soul here but locals, and not a man in the place who'd give a damn for an angry husband.'

The two were skilled practitioners of the 'badger game'. During the season, in this or one of a half-dozen similar resorts, married or prominent people, usually men, would find themselves in physical rapport with a charming girl, only to have their bliss shattered by the irruption of an angry husband. Most preferred to buy their way out of publicity. None ever made a fuss.

'Skip it,' the man said. 'We've enough put by for the winter. Hairy Mary's been giving me the eye again. I think I'll go and see if I can stand the strain this time.'

'Watch it. She'll suck you dry and blow you out in little bubbles.' There was no sexual jealousy within the partnership. Being brother and sister, they only needed each other that way when all else had failed.

'As good a way to go as any,' he replied, 'and better than some. What about you? Can I have the use of our place?'

'I suppose. There's a kid with a mean, intense look. Over by the pillar. One haircut and he'd be almost good-looking. He's taken me up four times. When he dances he gives out with the body language and I like what he's saying. I'll give him a tumble. This one's just for fun.'

'Fine,' her brother said. 'If the fish doesn't bite, go for a walk and then knock before you come in, right?'

'Right.'

She made an unnecessary trip to the ladies and on her return paused where Chas could hardly fail to see her, timing her arrival for the start of the next dance. They stood up together. The volume of music and the style of dancing hardly encouraged conversation but they exchanged tiny sexual messages. Chas played this game from habit and hope. Lust did not come quickly to him these days, nor let itself be sensed lurking. He had to assure himself that it would be there when it was wanted. The drug habit had aged him young.

'I'm hungry,' he said over the din.

She treated him to a bright and innocent smile. 'For what?' she shouted back.

He returned her smile. He had a nice smile when he cared to use it. 'Like food, for now,' he said. 'Let's get out of this racket.'

'There's a good Chinkie round the corner, stays open.'

He stood by while she collected a fluffy, artificial fur. They walked in close contact to a small restaurant which held a soft babble of sound but seemed quiet after the noise of the disco. They ate Chinese food, shared a bottle of wine and chatted superficially, searching for subjects in common. Chas found that she was badly educated but worldly-wise. She might be a worthy long-term prospect.

There were no taxis. They walked to his hotel. It was locked up but he had a key. They padded through the dusty corridors.

It was no love affair but a strict exchange of sexual gratification. This was tacitly understood by both. Stimulated by a change of flesh and voice and scent, and refreshed by his brief celibacy, Chas managed one quick coupling. Not all the tricks in her repertoire could rouse him again. But, she admitted appreciatively to herself, he was patient and resourceful. Although she would have preferred more conventional sex, a little variety never came amiss. Her appetite was assuaged at last.

So it was not unsatisfied carnality which woke her early but a personal habit. As the years stole the bloom of her youth she had learned not to let her lovers see her in the morning.

It was also from habit that she slipped his watch and wallet into her handbag. Chas was sleeping soundly on his back. She dressed quickly, ready for a quick departure if the regular popping sound which he made on each outward breath should cease, before searching the places which she knew from experience to be where men hid their valuables. Her first act was to slide out the bottom drawer of the chest. On the floor beneath, among some other clutter, was a wad of notes which made her blink. Rather than waste time in separating the valuable from the rubbish, she snaffled the lot.

Chas was bare to the waist. He would be cold when she opened the window. She pulled the duvet gently over his chest before she slipped away.

SEVEN

Sylvia did not allow herself to count the hours to Jimmy's return. He had, after all, said only that he would try to get back by Saturday evening. He might be delayed until Sunday morning. Or afternoon. Or whatever.

Rather than face a thousand disappointments, she let herself believe that she was encapsulated for ever in her up-market cell. She had her books and her music and her few domestic chores. She had furnishings of a value which she could only vaguely appreciate. And she had a whole variety of rich foods. She had found chocolates and sweets in plenty among the supplies. Jimmy's experience seemed to have been limited to girls with a sweet tooth.

This brought a fresh worry to mind. When she found that she had emptied the first chocolate box in little over an hour, she realised that idleness, stress and good food might soon combine to make her as fat as a pig. She despised fat women. She started a regime of such exercises as she could remember from her schooldays. She also decided to begin a diet, without going so far as to set a deadline for its start. Like many others, she found an escape from worry in eating.

Late on Saturday afternoon the click at the door and the spread of reflected light across the concrete ceiling caught her lying on her back and pedalling conscientiously with her feet overhead. With the end to her isolation and the sudden intrusion of the outside world her unease tried to float up again, but Jimmy's shy presence beyond the bars suppressed it.

'You been all right?' he asked anxiously.

'I've got by.' She saw that it was still dry outside although the light of day was failing already.

'I brought some more things.'

She looked into the cartons of food. 'I'm not half way through the last lot,' she said. 'You'll have me putting on weight.'

'You could do with some flesh on your bones,' he said bravely. He was not blushing so easily now.

'And I thought you thought I was perfect! And now you tell me I'm skinny. Do you think you can't have too much of a good thing?'

'Something like that. There's clothes too.'

'Bless you! But you needn't have bothered. I'll put them aside for when I need them.'

She was teasing him and he knew it but he pleased her by blushing again. 'Don't,' he said in a strangled voice.

'You mean you want . . . ?'

He nodded without meeting her eye.

'Later, if at all,' she said firmly. She felt that she must try to retain some kind of domination despite their roles. He mustn't look on her as if she were a canary in a cage. 'How long are you staying this time?'

'The evening if you want. Can't manage tomorrow but I'll be along on Monday. I brought the chess things if you'd like.'

'I'd like.'

'If I stayed the evening, would you . . . ?' He nodded to the floorspace between the bars and the first stack.

'You're getting to be a bit of a lad. We'll see,' she said. She hoped that she was not starting something which might rebound. 'Have you eaten?'

'Not since my dinner.'

'I'll put something on to cook while you bring your things in.'

She had to climb on a chair and put a bulb into the nearest lamp. They ate and then played chess into the evening. This time, although they both played badly, he was winning more games than he lost. Her mind kept straying from the geometric problems of the chessboard to her private disquiet. If Mr Daw was dishonest – and surely this was not an honest man's storehouse – why was he helping her? Chas could not be paying him the sort of money which would signify with such a man. And where was Chas? Where was The Irishman? There had been nothing on the news about his capture, but a suspected bomber had been reported in Glasgow who sounded very much like him. If The Irishman was in Glasgow, why couldn't she go home?

In the next game, when her queen was already in trouble, the thought which she had been burying deepest came bobbing to the surface, unbidden and unwelcome. If Mr Daw had shut her up with a cache of stolen goods of, she felt sure, enormous value, was he really going to let her go free to talk about it? Was he counting on her gratitude to keep her quiet? He could probably have done so, but did he know it?

'I'm sorry,' she said. 'I can't keep my mind on the game. Let's pack it in.'

He nodded and started to put the pieces into their box. 'Something bothering you?'

'I've been in here about a week already,' she said. 'That's enough to bother anybody. Do you know why I'm here?'

'None of my business,' he said.

'What do you think?'

'If I had to guess,' he said slowly, 'I'd think that you were in trouble that wasn't of your own making. Maybe that you'd been the girl of somebody important like a politician, and he wanted you out of the way for a bit. Until some question stopped being asked. Something like that.'

'You're away off. I'm not even sure if it's about what I

think it is. Will you be seeing Mr Daw tomorrow?'

He shook his head. 'Monday morning.'

'Would you ask him to let me know what's happening?'

Jimmy thought solemnly and then nodded. 'I could ask. He wouldn't mind being asked. Not to say that he'd answer, though.'

'At least it might remind him that I'm here.'

'Doesn't need reminding,' Jimmy said. 'He knows you're here. Asked me if I'd remembered to bring you food.'

'Well, ask him anyway,' Sylvia said. 'Jimmy, you know what I'd like most of all?'

'What?'

'I'd like to take a walk outside in the fresh air. Stretch my legs. I wouldn't be any trouble.'

He shook his head emphatically. 'I would if I could. But Mr Daw keeps the key of the gate on his ring and never puts it down. Never lets me have it either. Too much valuable stuff in here.'

'Including me?'

'P'raps.'

'And there's not another key somewhere?'

'Not that I know of.'

Sylvia was not going to be beaten. 'If you brought in some tools, couldn't you unbolt the lock or the hinges or something?'

He smiled at the ignorance of females. 'No chance! It's all welded.'

'Can you pick a lock?'

'Don't know. I never tried.'

'Jimmy, I'm getting desperate,' she said and was surprised by the depth of feeling in her own voice. 'If I don't get a breath of fresh air and a bit of a walk and focus on something that's more than a few feet away, I think I'll go mad. Couldn't you look for another key?

And, failing that, bring whatever you need and see if you can't pick the lock?'

He thought about it in such silence that she could hear her own heartbeat and breathing. 'I'd be risking the sack,' he said at last. 'I'd never get another job like this one. And I already done you favours. Time you did something for me.'

Sylvia misunderstood. So far, he had been so easily satisfied. 'You want to watch me again, is that it?'

'More than that,' he said breathlessly. 'You know.'

She was neither surprised nor shocked. In fact, the bargain seemed fair. 'You'd have to get the gate open first,' she said.

'If I get the sack, I mightn't be able to come back at all,' he said. 'I can't promise to get the gate open. I can only try. This is for trying. We could manage. Now.'

'And you'd promise?'

'I'd promise to try. That's all I could do, isn't it?'

'That's true.' She thought that, with the bars between them, the same applied to her own side of the bargain.

Now that they were agreed, he took command. She was the one who was embarrassed. She felt shy, undressing under the overhead light. He kept his clothes on but unzipped his fly.

Face to face and through the bars it was impossible. It would have been impossible even if he had not been clumsy with inexperience. Fruitless efforts were not unfamiliar to her, but to him they were the end of the world. She would have treated him to fellatio, but the idea seemed to scandalise him.

'We could manage if you turned round,' he said.

Having come so far, it seemed very little further. She turned and stood with her hands on her knees and he entered her at last. The bars scraped her buttocks and made his penetration shallow.

'Look at the floor and think of home,' she told herself

wryly. She did not expect pleasure but she found that she was sharing his enjoyment. He was a virgin of around twenty years with a lot of energy to expend and nature had been more lavish to him than to Chas. At the height of her pleasure she remembered that he had never kissed her.

She thought that it was an odd way to preserve her domination, presenting her bottom to him. Perhaps dependence would suffice. The blood was running to her head. She had only her own feet to look at, and the concrete floor.

God, but it was better than it had ever been with Chas!

When they finished, he thanked her politely. A few minutes later he locked the door and left her. This time, he did not ask to watch her dress.

Jimmy walked up the road, whistling. He would try, as he had promised. But he was not going to put his job on the line. She had no more to offer him now. He hoped that his mother would not be able to see the glow which encircled his loins.

EIGHT

On Monday morning, Nelson Daw decided to attend Jimmy's morning session in the back lane. Although Jimmy had become almost autonomous, and Daw could tell from the balance of receipts against expenditure that he was honest, Daw liked to remind the boy occasionally that he was an employee and not self-employed.

They waited in the van, snug in their almost secret cul-de-sac. A petty thief brought some brand-new calculators and digital watches which had found their way out of the back door of a discount warehouse. Otherwise all was quiet.

Jimmy stood in awe of his employer, but during one of the silences he got up his nerve to speaking point. 'The girl, Mr Daw,' he said suddenly. 'What's her future?'

Daw's mind had been far away, teasing over the problems of giving himself a tax-free and untraceable income. Money could be laundered very effectively in London by way of Certificates of Possession of Gold, and Dutch private banks made their Swiss colleagues look garrulous by comparison, but still . . . He dragged his mind back. 'Future?'

'She keeps asking me when she's getting out of there.'

'You can't tell her what you don't know.'

'I'd like to tell her something.'

'Tell her that it could be several weeks yet.' Daw turned his head and looked at Jimmy. 'Don't tell me that you're falling for her!'

Jimmy flushed. 'Not exactly.'

In his cold way, Daw was fond of the boy. More

importantly, a romance between the two could be a danger. 'My advice is to stay at arm's length from her,' he said. 'Leave food, take away refuse. Say nothing and above all don't answer any questions.'

'Yes, Mr Daw,' Jimmy said.

'You'll learn,' the fence said kindly. 'Getting involved with people doesn't pay. Be kind, be respected, but don't be involved. Give all your loyalty to your associates and your family. Take a woman to yourself some day and make her part of that family. Outside of those groups, you won't have enough love and loyalty to go round. Look at it this way. The world's full of people who need money. But if you tried to give each of them a penny, how far would you get? And how much would it mean to them? The same goes for every other sort of need. So think of every outsider as being no more than a chessman. You understand me?'

'Yes, Mr Daw.'

'You don't, but you will. Find yourself a nice girl. Before you let yourself fall for her, make sure that there aren't any born losers in her family. Then give her everything and expect the same in return. That one in the store, she's not for you. She's not for anybody. She's a commodity. She's goods for buying and selling. You asked about her future.'

'Yes.'

'She doesn't have one. Don't tell her that. She'll be a lot more trouble when she finds it out. I'm trusting you,' Daw said sharply.

'I know it,' Jimmy said under his breath.

Nelson Daw was putting more trust in the fact that the only key to the barred gate was on the ring in his pocket, but it did no harm to remind the boy now and again where his loyalties lay.

Sylvia had made up her mind that if she could get Jimmy to open the doors she would run for it. If she could get among people she would surely be safe from re-capture by the inexperienced boy.

She broke her own rule and counted the hours, and on Monday Jimmy never came. She played music at full volume. She paced the alleyways between the stacks. She lay on the camp bed and forced herself to read, only to find that she was sucking her thumb again. Her sleep that night was disturbed by dreams – ominous dreams, she knew, although she could never remember them.

Late on the Tuesday morning she heard the familiar sounds and saw the change in the light. She ran to the bars. Jimmy was putting down a single carton of food and she was almost relieved to see that he had not heaped her with luxuries again.

'You didn't come, yesterday,' she said.

He was slow to meet her eye. 'Couldn't,' he said. 'I was left in charge of the shop while the boss went to a sale. I knew you'd got enough food. Can't stop long today either. We won't get our chess.'

'I'd rather have a walk in the open air,' she said. 'Did you find a key?'

'No. But I tried. I did try. He left me in the shop on my own and I went through the office. If there's another key, it's in the safe and he definitely has the only key to that.'

'Did you speak to him?'

'He couldn't tell me anything.'

'Couldn't or wouldn't?' she asked.

'Don't know. I'll have to go soon.'

Her hopes were dying one by one. 'Aren't you going to try to pick this lock?'

He shook his head.

'But you promised!' she wailed.

'Look, if I did I wouldn't have time to take you for a walk,' he said. 'Leave it to tomorrow.'

'And tomorrow you won't turn up again. I'm beginning to see what your promises are worth.' She was close to tears. She should have been playing the seductress.

She knew that she sounded more like a spoiled child but she could not stop. 'You got what you wanted and now you don't want to do anything in return. You're just a . . . ' She broke off. She could not think what he was.

To Jimmy, the lack of the word somehow made her rebuke worse. He knew what he was. He sighed ostentatiously. 'I'll try,' he said and turned to the door. 'Nag, nag, nag,' his voice drifted back.

He brought back some tools from the van, a hacksaw and some wire, and fashioned two hooks with which he probed unhopefully at the innards of the complicated lock.

'It beats me,' he said at last.

Sylvia had had time to cool down and to sense his attitude. 'There's something you're not telling me, isn't there?'

He bent quickly to the lock again. 'No, there's nothing.'

'Yes there is. I can tell. What is it? Something about The Irishman?'

This time he could look at her in genuine incomprehension. 'I don't know anything about no Irishman,' he said.

'Well, there's something. Tell me. Tell me, Jimmy.'

'There's nothing,' he said. 'Got to go now.'

'When will you be back?'

'Don't know.' He picked up his tools. 'Here! Where's my hacksaw?' She was standing awkwardly with one hand behind her back. 'You give me that.'

'Not a chance,' she said, backing away.

He stood and glared at her while his mind worked. He might lack confidence but he could be very logical. 'It'd take you an hour to cut them bars,' he said. 'And then you'd have two more doors to get through, and a hacksaw wouldn't be much good for either of them. I can be back with Mr Daw in half an hour easy, and he'll open up the gate and go after you. Now, you gimme that hacksaw or I'll lock up and go for him.'

Sylvia's courage wilted at the thought of sawing against time while waiting for the arrival of an angry Mr Daw. She handed over the hacksaw. Jimmy threw it behind him and grabbed her wrist. 'What about the other thing?' he asked hoarsely.

'You're out of your mind,' Sylvia said. 'You haven't done what you promised and you treat me like shit and you expect – Hey!' He had turned her with her back against the bars and was holding her there with one arm. 'Cut it out. You can't rape me through these bars.'

'I bloody can,' he said, fumbling at his trousers with his spare hand.

'If you do,' she said, 'I'll jump sideways and chop you off. Snap you like a carrot!'

She felt his tumescence wither and he let her go. He backed away, pulling up his zip. She smoothed her skirt down. Neither said anything. He picked up the tools and went, locking the doors behind him.

She went back to her own corner of the basement and in a surge of fury she threw the jade figure against the wall. It did little to relieve her feelings so she gathered up the fragments and dropped them down the drain. Then she lay down on the camp bed and tried to control her tears.

NINE

Somebody, in Liverpool or Glasgow, had talked. The Irishman, after his first lapse, had moved through the urban jungles with the stealth of a stoat in undergrowth. But there was an Identikit picture of somebody who might have been mistaken for him, on display in post offices and elsewhere. The face, which was too thin by far, was shown with and without a beard, but the beard shown was far more bushy than his neat little brush. He presumed that it was his cousin's work or that it had been composed from hearsay and that danger was not too immediate.

The post offices, his favourite targets, were being watched. He cadged some plastique from an acquaintance in a not dissimilar line of business and opened the safe in a small pawnbroker's shop. The haul produced some gold trinkets and a disappointing amount of cash. After sending off a repayment to his cousin, because, after all, family was family, he had only a few pounds to line his own pocket.

Cities with a high Irish content were evidently being searched for him. On the other hand, home might have cooled down by now if the false trails were being followed. Anyway, he had been too long away from his ex-barmaid.

He hitch-hiked out of Liverpool and spent the pawnbroker's money on a journey five times as long as necessary, by coach, night train and three different buses, changing his clothes and his walk along the way and arriving near home in mid-morning. He had never expected to think it about a place outside of Ireland, but he was glad to be back.

His small beard had filled out now and he had let his sideburns grow. Dyed a deeper black, they broadened his face and he had increased the effect by a little padding in his cheeks. A thin cushion padded out his hollow chest and wedges of newspaper in his shoes affected his walk. If he could have guarded his tongue, he thought, he might have been careful all the time. He was certainly careful now.

From a street which ran parallel to his own he could see the back of the flats. There was no blue vase in her kitchen window. Either she had forgotten his instructions already, in which case he would take a stick to her, or she was not sure that it would be safe for him to visit.

He rounded two corners to a phone box, dialled her number and waited with a coin at the ready. Her voice answered, the rapid pips took over and he dropped his money. He could detect no sign of phone tapping but he decided to play it safe.

'Is that two-four-seven-two?' he asked, reading the number off the phone in front of him. All trace of Ireland was carefully excluded from his voice.

'I'm afraid that you have a wrong number,' she said carefully, and disconnected.

Soon he saw her coming from the direction of the flats, pushing the pram and waddling on her unsuitable heels. She walked past without a glance towards him. A smile spread inside him. She might be as dumpling in mind as she was in body, but she had learned from him after all. Nobody followed her. He gave her time to get to the box by the Benefit Office and then put his hand on the phone. It rang and he picked it up.

'Is that you, Sean dear?'

'It is, my love. Are they watching the place?'

'They've been to see me twice,' she said placidly. 'I

said I didn't know the man who lived opposite, except to pass him on the stairs, and I'd never looked him in the face at all. But a flat across the street just changed hands, and never a minute passes without a face near the window.'

'Is your phone tapped?'

'It went off for a while after the first visit.'

'That does it, then,' he said. 'Time we weren't here. I'll get money and passports together and we'll get away abroad. Somewhere the sun shines. You'd like that?'

'Anywhere with you, Sean. As long as it's somewhere little Pat can be brought up safely and well.'

'You're a good girl. You'll not hear from me for a while. But be ready to move the moment I make contact again. Then, don't argue, just do what I say and when. Are you all right for money?'

'Not too bad, Sean dear. And I've a message for you.' He could almost hear her wrinkling her smooth forehead with effort. Memory had never come easily to her. 'You must speak to Sailor Jackbird right away. It's important for both of you.'

It took him only a second to translate Sailor Jackbird into Nelson Daw. 'I was thinking of paying him a call,' he said. 'Look after yourself, me darlin'. I could just be doing with an hour between those plump thighs of yours.'

'I'd like that too,' she said. She went on to mention certain desires which, when he left the box, distorted his walk still further until he managed to re-arrange himself.

Nelson Daw was alone in his shop. He seemed to be studying the scene outside. The glass had all been replaced and the only physical scar on the town was the gap and the shoring where once had been his favourite pub.

But there was another mark on the town. The bomb, by selecting the lunchtime drinkers, had taken out family heads, breadwinners, kingpins of business or local politics or of local society. In that sense it would never be the same place again. Daw was glad to be leaving.

Even so, things were moving too fast for his peace of mind. Gollen Manor had changed hands only a few months before, but the new owner had died before he could take occupation. The executors had known that their late client had outbid the next offerer by a sizeable margin. Public tender was therefore unlikely to produce any bids to match what Daw was offering, so they had decided to grab for his money before he could change his mind. With deeds recently drawn up, searches of title completed and surveys available, the lawyers had moved at a speed which surprised everybody and astonished themselves. On the previous day, Daw had closed the shop and travelled to a solicitor's office, to sign a new name to the contract and to write, in a pristine chequebook, a cheque whose size appalled him.

It had been one thing, he found, to follow his well-grooved routines while planning the giant step somewhere in the remote future. It was quite another to part with almost half of his accumulated assets and a considerably larger proportion of his available cash. The lawyers' fees, also, had increased the total by a staggering margin. It was time to clear his treasure house. Fortunately, the manor was well provided with secure outbuildings from which he could despatch his treasures to foreign buyers already earmarked.

He was casting his mind over his other assets with such concentration that when one of them walked into the shop he failed to recognise it.

'Good morning, sir,' he said. He could be properly unctuous when the occasion demanded. 'Can I show you something?'

'If you've a bottle, you could show me a bit of hospitality.'

Daw peered at him. 'Good God, Irishman! Is that you? I'd never have known you.'

'I should hope not indeed.'

'Come into the office before somebody more perceptive arrives.'

They settled down in the hard chairs. Daw watched the shop through the one-way mirror. From the shop side, it appeared to be a wall-hung, Georgian mirror with a gilt frame. Several customers had tried the frame with a pin, to see whether it was the original oak under the gilding or an Edwardian copy. It was, in fact, glass-fibre.

He produced a bottle of Irish whiskey which he had put by for the occasion. A little loosening of The Irishman's tongue might help him to play his cards. They began with a glass each while he paid cash for the pawnbroker's gold. He refilled The Irishman's glass. His own was hardly touched.

'You've made this country too hot for you, Irishman,' he said. He spoke without anger. His insurers had more than made up his losses. The fact that he might very easily have been in that pub at the moment when the bomb went off was neither here nor there. On the wrong side of the law, there is little room for the might-have-been. 'What you need is money and a passport. Get yourself and your woman abroad.'

'That's what I was thinking myself.'

Daw opened his small safe, took out a bundle o passports and thumbed through them. His clients al knew that there was a ready market for stolen passports He held one up, open at the photograph. 'How woul that suit you? Grow a handlebar moustache instead o that beard, give your woman spectacles and explain tha she's put on weight, and that's the pair of you to a T.'

'How much?'

'I've six safes lined up for you. Do those and I'll thro in the passports.' He had only three safes in mind and on of those was doubtful, but he could buy information on a few more while The Irishman was busy with the first.

'And what might your own percentage be?' The Irishman asked keenly.

Daw filled the other's glass again. 'You'd better put that down you,' he said. 'You're in for a shock.' He put a cassette into the dictation machine on his desk and pressed the Play button.

The Irishman listened, outwardly impassively, to Sylvia's voice. 'I saw a man . . . attaché case . . . I knew him for sure . . .'

'That's the bird belongs to young Chas,' he said when it finished. 'The Cantor girl. Where is she?'

'I have her safely stowed away,' Daw said. 'Open all six safes and you get her and the passport thrown in with your cut of the last one. Let me down and you get no passport and the girl goes to the police. My cut's eighty per cent.'

'Seventy,' The Irishman said.

'Seventy-five.'

'Done,' The Irishman said. A quarter of the contents of six safes and a sound passport would see them safely abroad. Daw never wasted time chasing after rubbish. And if he could find as good a passport elsewhere, he'd keep the whole of the last haul.

'You'll not regret it. The girl must die, mind,' Daw said anxiously. 'She's seen too much.'

The Irishman only nodded. It went without saying. 'I'll need somewhere to stay. They're watching my place.'

Daw thought about it. 'Young Chas is out of town,' he said. 'He thought you might be after him for selling me the girl.'

'I'm grateful to him. You got the key?'

'If you can open a safe you can surely slip a lock,' Daw said. 'I'll write down the address.'

Chas was suffering as he was doomed to suffer and perhaps more. His spoon and syringe had been in the sponge-bag which he had bought to hold his new toiletries. With them had been an opened sachet of his drug, containing no more than a day's dosage. That bitch had lifted all the rest.

By cutting his dose and suffering accordingly, Chas had given himself two days to find the girl and beg back his stock; or to find money and another source of supply.

But the girl, wisely, had vanished. Chas could find no trace of her except for the faint shadow of a knowing smile when he asked questions about her. He could have bought heroin if he had money, but addicts are seldom given credit and the dealer was not interested in being paid in stolen goods.

He gave up at last. His shaking hands and running nose and eyes were calling attention to him and making successful theft impossible, even if he had known of a safe fence in the town.

The woman had not even left him his fare home bu she had missed the collection of keys in the bottom of hi old duffel bag. He quitted the hotel during the nigh leaving a substantial bill unpaid, and helped himself to car which had been parked on the seafront. Its tank wa almost empty. He removed the bulb from the tail-ligh and found an all-night, self-service petrol station wher he parked abreast of the attendant, filled up and drov off quickly. He stopped only to re-instate his lights an drove on through several roundabouts. Nobody bothere him.

He was glad to abandon the car at the railway station half a mile from home. His condition had made driving nightmare. Apart from the physical pangs of withdrawa his inner mind was throwing up images of huge insect appearing out of nowhere and sometimes vanishing a abruptly. He had once signalled and pulled out overtake a ten-foot-high ladybird. Realising that this was no more than a hallucination, he had resolved to ignore the larger bluebottle which was hogging the road ahead of the ladybird, only to see the bluebottle become a very real articulated lorry. He could only be thankful that his guardian angel, who had never done him any other favours that he could remember, had chosen that night to make up for past neglect.

He threaded the streets towards Daw's shop, pacing carefully and holding his face still so as not to draw attention to himself. Daw was with a customer. He took one look at Chas's face and gestured him through into the office where he joined him a few minutes later.

'I've seen happier-looking corpses,' Daw said. 'Often. Vhat happened to you?'

'I got rolled.'

'The whole bundle and your drugs?'

'Yeah.'

'That's tough. But what do you expect me to do about t?'

'I can't operate in this condition,' Chas said. He was tating the obvious. 'Lend me enough to get fixed and I'll ring you a whole lot of stuff within a couple of days.'

'You know my rule,' Daw said. 'Goods first, cash nmediately after. The Irishman's staying at your place. 'harge him for his board.'

Chas accepted the news without excitement. Among is other troubles, what was an Irish bomber? 'Has he ot any money?' he asked.

'I shouldn't think so, by now.' Daw had not paid much r the golden trinkets, and The Irishman would have ocked up with food and whisky before moving in.

'The rent's due tomorrow,' Chas said, 'and they've en gunning for me. If it's not paid, there'll be bailiffs with a man to change the lock. I was going to post em the rent, but now I can't.'

Daw sighed. 'How much?'

'Twenty-five would cover it.'

Daw produced two ten pound notes and a fiver. He could always deduct it from The Irishman's first share. 'This is for the rent,' he said, 'not for hopping yourself up. Come right back with the receipt or I'll give our friend the same to flatten you.' Another idea came to him. 'If you want to make a couple of hundred for yourself, tell me where there's a safe worth having him open.'

'If I knew that,' Chas said, 'I'd get into it myself if I had to chew my way inside it.'

He blew his nose and wiped his eyes and set off for the rent office. Roughcast was being renewed along the frontage and he had to pass under scaffolding to get in at the door. He refused to bandy words with the cashier, who was delighted to see him in such poor shape. When he emerged, the creatures of his mind gave him a brief respite and he saw something which he had seen without registering on the way in.

Typically, he made contact with Fat Alec before hurrying back to the antique shop.

TEN

'Uncle' Joe Sulliman was known, to the few who had ever seen him without his bowler hat, to be as bald as the proverbial egg. This was his only lack. He was a large man, comfortably and expensively stout; his blue suits and his large, black shoes had to be made for him. He typified the jolly old gentleman, everybody's uncle, to the point beyond which nobody ever gave him the second glance which might have shown them that his eyes were cold.

Uncle had been a courier all his working life. He had never known the stigma of unemployment. There is always a market for the man who can deliver the goods safely, promptly and honestly. Even as a young man, before settled conditions and firm laws ruined the white slave trade, his avuncular manner was a comfort to the young ladies whom he escorted to those parts of the world which were plagued by excessive male immigration. Later, he had transported illicit gemstones, illegal immigrants and armaments.

He had come late into the drug scene but thrived in it. The rings which employed him might be broken and re-formed but Uncle sailed on in his calm and smiling way. He was too wary to trap and too patently honest to suspect.

But he was more than a mere courier for Britain's largest and longest surviving drug ring. He was an entrepreneur. Nobody was better placed to gather up and weave together the threads of information which permeate the criminal world. The various local dealers who depended on him for their supplies sought his favour by collecting scraps of gossip for him. A socialite addict, desperate for relief and cut off from her allowance, might in her turn be favoured if she let slip the date when mummy's famous emeralds would be out of the bank and into daddy's safe. At the other end of the country, a new customer might turn out to have a talent for opening that very make of safe. The art of management is the matching of the man to the task, ensuring that he is fully informed and leaving him to get on with it. Uncle would have shone in the upper echelons of some great enterprise. But he preferred to take a percentage rather than a salary.

This sideline was well known to Uncle's employers, although they may not have realised its scope. They tolerated it because Uncle never took a risk and because a courier who was never short of money was the courier to be trusted.

His third and last activity was as a salesman of double-glazing. This was no more than a cover and on the rare occasions when he was forced to make a sale nobody was more surprised than the manufacturer who had never heard of him. His sample cases and literature had been stolen from one of their representatives and modified to suit Uncle's purposes.

Uncle covered a lot of miles in the year, mostly by British Rail. While Sylvia was fretting in Nelson Daw' care, Uncle made his eighth visit of the year to Aberdeen Even on the face of it, this looked reasonable. The col northern city, bombarded by the noise of helicopter an other traffic from Dyce Airport, was a healthy market fo double-glazing. More to his point, the oil industry ha brought traffic into Aberdeen Harbour with which th over-stretched Customs and Excise was quite unable t cope.

In the bar of His Majesty's Theatre he had made h

contact with the mate of a Dutch tug and, without a word being said, they had exchanged fat briefcases by placing them on separate tables, visiting the bar and each returning to the other's table. Uncle had made his first delivery before he left the theatre.

Next morning, with his sample cases weighted by the plastic packets behind their false backs, he took the train south to Dundee where his next delivery was due. He met his contact, a part-time barman, for lunch in an Indian restaurant. The food was terrible, so bad that not even students would eat it. The choice of venue was Uncle's. The quality of the food helped to keep his weight down and also ensured a degree of privacy.

'Well now, Hughie,' he said when the proprietor and his whole family had withdrawn after serving them. 'Tell me what's been going on in your neck of the woods.'

'Not a lot,' Hughie said, 'from what I hear.'

Uncle nodded. As a barman as well as a dealer, Hughie would hear. 'It's quiet all over just now,' he said.

'The police have been more active than anyone else.'

Uncle pricked up his ears. 'How's that?' he said.

'Some false alarm about an Irish bomber coming up this way.'

'Oh, that,' Uncle said. 'It was on the news. False alarm, was it?'

'The Irish were saying he's never been near the place. But there are posters up, and a reward.'

'Is that so?' Uncle turned the subject. But he was interested enough to call at a post office and to study one of the posters. The pictures could have represented almost anybody, but among the aliases quoted he recognised more than one. He caught his train to Edinburgh in thoughtful mood. He had recently had word of a high-quality safe in a solicitor's office through which a large sum in cash was to pass soon, ultimately destined for the corruption of a high official in the

Middle East, but competent safe-blowers seemed to be in short supply at the moment.

He was well known in his small Edinburgh hotel. He had established his identity years before by holding a double-glazing seminar there, so that the staff were not in the least surprised by the usual trickle of businesslike men, each presenting an appropriate card. Uncle was meeting his premier customers in Scotland's industrial central belt.

The man from Glasgow came last and they adjourned to the bar for a sociable drink.

'Well, Dougal my boy,' Uncle said. 'What's this I hear about Wilf Connors, or whatever he calls himself now, being up Dundee way?'

Dougal grinned, showing a hideous set of dentures. An Irish Glaswegian, he had been a welder in a Clydeside shipyard until an accident had cost him his teeth and his job. He thought that it had been worth it. He was one of the very few dealers who used their own commodity, but Uncle liked and trusted him all the same.

'He was in Glasgow,' Dougal said. 'That I do know. From what I hear, Dundee was a red herring.'

'The fuzz seem to have bought it,' Uncle said. 'The place was plastered with posters about him.'

'They didn't altogether buy it. My nephew in Liverpool knows him. He says the man turned up there but the coppers were waiting for him and he's on the run now. If he doesn't get caught going back for his woman, he'll try to get abroad. Have to.'

'I expect you're right,' Uncle said.

Chas was awake, very early by his standards and in more misery that he would have believed possible. On top of his withdrawal symptoms, which had reached a new peak, was the aftermath of the beating which The Irishman had given him the night before.

Chas had claimed his two hundred pounds from Nelson Daw, made his purchase from Fat Alec and stumbled home. Daw had assured him that The Irishman was properly grateful to him for taking Sylvia out of circulation, and Chas had prepared to give his guest a friendly word before dashing to the bathroom and pacifying his body with a dose of narcotics now three days overdue.

Instead, he had found himself confronted by a madman, three parts drunk and one part furious, who demanded to know where Sylvia was hidden and then, refusing to believe that Chas did not know the answer, had announced his intention of beating it out of him.

The Irishman's reputation as a hard man had proved to be a true bill. He seemed to know every painful, paralysing nerve in the human body. Chas, too feeble to offer a real resistance, had made the mistake of lashing out blindly and had caught the other on one of his always sensitive ears. From that moment The Irishman had abandoned his quest for knowledge and had concentrated on reducing Chas to a pulp until unconsciousness intervened.

Chas found himself to be on his own bed, still clothed. He wondered whether his new clothes were bloodstained but could not raise his head to see. He tried to let time pass. The pain from his beating was a pinprick compared to the agonies of withdrawal. Some day he might feel well enough to make it as far as the bathroom, and that was enough of a goal in life.

When he saw The Irishman looming over him, Chas gave an involuntary heave which re-doubled all his pains.

But The Irishman seemed to be in a more pacific mood. 'Don't you be trying to move yourself,' he said, feeling as you do. I won't be bothering you again about the girl.'

Chas found that he had just enough strength to speak. 'Mean that?' he croaked.

'Surely I do. I believe you now. If you'd known where she was, you'd have told me. Up you get now. You'll feel better with some breakfast inside you.'

'Huh!' Chas said.

'You don't look too great and that's a fact,' The Irishman said. 'Is there anything I can get you?'

Chas lifted one hand and mimed pumping an injection into the other arm.

'That's what it is, is it? Sure, I'll do that much for you. I know what it's like to need the hair of the dog.'

Under Chas's whispered instructions, The Irishman sterilised water and the spoon, measured and mixed the dose and held the tourniquet while Chas fumbled for the vein. Chas closed his eyes and kept silence while the drug did its work. After his abstinence, the effect was quicker and stronger. In ten minutes, as the withdrawal symptoms faded, he could distinguish the pains from his trouncing, and even those were soothed. He thought that he might be smiling.

'That's better,' The Irishman said. 'Come along now and we'll get you into a hot bath and soak away some of the bruising. I'll be like a mother to you. Better than that. If your ma was here, she'd tan your arse for getting into a fight with the likes of me.'

He was as good as his word. He ran a hot bath, half-carried Chas into the bathroom, undressed him and lowered him tenderly into the water. He went so far as to sponge those parts of Chas which appeared above the surface. Then, while Chas steeped some more of his pains away, he went and made mugs of hot, sweet tea and brought them into the bathroom, seating himself companionably on the toilet bowl and helping Chas to drink. Chas, who had not eaten for more than a day found that once he managed to start swallowing he could hardly bear to stop.

'Two pals such as we are shouldn't fall out over a woman,' The Irishman said. Chas looked up sharply but he was perfectly serious. 'Tell me, young Chas, do I remember, or is it my drunken dreams talking, that while we were having our little altercation last night you were trying to tell me something about Mr Daw having a job for me?'

'I was,' Chas said. 'But I think it's too late now.'

'Is that so? Tell me about it anyway.'

The horrors of the night and morning were ebbing, leaving behind the flotsam of reality. Chas concentrated on stringing the words together. 'Today's rent day. The local rent office collects from about three thousand tenants. Most of them aren't the sort to write cheques. When the pay packets go round, the wives collect the money from their men and go straight to the rent office with it. That's rent and rates together. Most of them pay between twenty and forty quid, depending on the size of house and whether they rent a garage.'

Chas paused to drink more tea. The Irishman did sums in his head. He seemed impressed. 'Is it a hold-up you're suggesting?'

'Most of it comes in late, after the bank's closed. They think it's less of a risk to keep it in the safe under the eye of the burglar alarms than to fetch it along to the bank's night safe after dark. I've seen security guards collecting the money in the morning. The water's getting cold,' Chas added plaintively.

The Irishman obligingly ran in some more hot water. 'What sort of alarms?' he asked.

'The new ones. Infra-red sensors picking up any moving heat source and a box on the wall outside with an electronic siren and a strobe light.'

'And if you cut a wire or open the box, it makes a noise to wake the devil and a light to blind him,' The Irishman said disgustedly. 'Unless you've got the key, I'll not touch it.'

'Let me finish,' Chas said. 'They're roughcasting the outside. The box is there, but it's just hanging on hooks until they finish. And there's enough surface cable that you could lift the box on to the flat roof. There's a great heap of sand in the car park at the back. All you'd have to do would be to dump enough sand over it, and it could make its noise and flash its little light all it wanted, nobody could see or hear it.'

'You're sure it's not connected right into the station?'

'Almost certain,' Chas said. 'It's sited so that they could see the light from the station. They wouldn't have bothered, if it was wired direct.'

'And how do I get inside?'

'Rooflight.'

'You wouldn't happen to remember the make of the safe?'

'No.'

'Too bad.' The Irishman went away and made more tea. When he came back with fresh mugs, he said, 'It sounds good. Get this down you and then up you come and into your clothes. You're going to draw me a plan. I'll study it while you take some breakfast and if it still looks good you can go and do some shopping. Maybe you could find some daft question to ask at the rent office while you read the maker's name on the safe.'

'I can't go out like this,' Chas protested.

'Well, I sure as hell can't,' The Irishman said. 'And it's not as if your marks would show. Stop the whining now. Your face is no worse than if you'd the toothache. Here's the best towel I could find.'

'You'll have to give me some money,' Chas said.

'And haven't you the wallet still full of the stuff?

never touched a penny of it,' The Irishman added quickly. 'I'll pay you back after I've done the job.'

'And Mr Daw said that you'd pay me a rent.'

'Pay you rent is it?' The Irishman demanded indignantly. 'It is you that should be paying me as an Irish au pair, and me scrubbing away like an old charwoman to try and make the place fit for a decent man to live in. What kind of a housekeeper that girl of yours was I'll never know. She'll be better dead.'

ELEVEN

Chas went through hell doing The Irishman's shopping. He could have lain still in comparative comfort, sat up with only minor pain. But not even the lift from his renewed drugging made him fit for walking. His ribs and stomach muscles seemed to have taken the brunt of the violence, but his thigh muscles also pained him and he was none too sure of his kidneys. His walk and his swollen jaw attracted looks which he could well have done without. He plodded through his errands numbly, without conscious thought.

He arrived back at the flat in early afternoon, to find a savoury smell conquering the older odours. Whatever his faults, The Irishman could cook.

'I think I got it all,' Chas said.

'You better.'

Chas started emptying his carrier bags on to the kitchen worktop. 'Nitric acid,' he said. 'Sulphuric acid.'

'You didn't get any two of them at the same shop?'

'Only things like bowls. Sugar. Photographic thermometer in centigrade. Glass bowls. Glass tubes. Glass funnel with as long a stem as I could get. Plasticine. Small glass marbles. Salt. Glycerine.'

'Did you have to go to the soapworks for it?'

'No. One of the chemists had it. Sodium carbonate That's the lot.'

'Timer and detonator I've got,' The Irishman said patting his pocket carefully. 'You can never get them when you want them in a hurry. Now sit down, lad. Ea first, work after, that's my rule.' He started to serve hi fragrant stew.

Chas's stomach wanted to rebel, but after the first few mouthfuls he was ravenously hungry and pleased The Irishman by wanting more. When they had finished, they washed up. Chas had never seen the kitchen so clean or tidy.

The Irishman opened all the windows in the flat. A cold breeze swept through the kitchen and made its exit through the window above the sink. 'That's good,' The Irishman said cheerfully. 'Drink makes you more likely to take the headaches. I don't know what drugs do. If you feel your head going, tell me and then go and hang out of the bedroom window.' He mixed his acids in one of the glass bowls, ran water into the sink and set the bowl in the water. 'That's fine,' he said. 'Sixteen degrees, near as makes no odds.' He warmed the jar of glycerine in a pan of hot water. 'I'll be running this in at thirty degrees. Your job's to keep the mixture between twenty-two and twenty-five. If it gets above twenty-five warn me and run the cold tap. If it gets to thirty, we run like hell.' He began to add the warm glycerine, mixing the liquids by blowing down a glass tube. The thermometer settled at twenty-three.

'OK?' The Irishman asked.

'So far,' Chas said. 'What are we doing?'

'Making nitroglycerine. What'd you think? Pay attention and you'll be able to do it by yourself next time. Now, we stand back and let it settle for a minute or two. If the job didn't have to be done tonight,' The Irishman said, 'I'd have gone looking for something safer, like RDX. But I used all I had in those parcels you took to London. I see they only used six,' he added. 'I wonder what they did with the other. If we had it now we could have saved ourselves the trouble.'

Only then did Chas remember the hidden attaché case. He opened his mouth and shut it again. The

Irishman was not patient with fools. Besides, he still felt that he might turn it into an asset some day.

The Irishman lifted the bowl on to the draining-board. Chas put his hand out to let the water out of the sink. 'Leave it,' the other said quickly. 'If one of us spills this bowl, the last thing we want is for the nitro to have a fall of thirty feet inside the waste-pipe. It'd flatten this building and the ones each side. A drop of three or four feet's usually enough to set it off. Now, you can see the line between the two liquids. That's spent acid on the bottom and nitro on top.' He was building a spout of plasticine on the rim of the bowl. When it was ready he began to decant the upper layer very carefully into the other bowl. When the line of demarcation neared the level of the spout, he began instead to decant into a clean jam jar and let the mixture settle again. He repeated the operation with a wine glass. When he was sure that his separation of the two liquids was as complete as he could make it, he straightened his back.

'You can get rid of the spent acid now,' he said. 'Add it to the sink water, pull the plug and flush it well away.'

Chas did as he was told. 'What now?' he asked. He was becoming interested despite his fears.

The Irishman was already making up another mixture. 'Like this,' he said, 'the mixture's still full of dissolved acids. Very dangerous. Here's where the sodium carbonate comes in.' He ran his solution into the bowl, mixed the liquids thoroughly by blowing air bubbles through and then began the process of separation over again. 'When you do this for yourself,' he said, 'think what you're at. This time, the nitro's on the bottom and the water's on top.'

'I'll remember,' Chas said. 'And where does the sugar come in?'

'It doesn't. I like my tea sweet.'

'I'll put it away. What about the salt?'

'Oh God!' The Irishman said. 'The ignorance of youth! Leave the salt where it is. We do the last wash in a strong brine. After that, it's safe as long as nobody breathes near it. You can put the kettle on, now. When it boils, don't bring it over here. It's for tea.'

When the last, delicate decanting was finished to The Irishman's satisfaction he had Chas hold a screw-top bottle while he poured his finished product carefully in through the funnel, never allowing a drop to fall but always running it down the glass. 'Nearly there,' he said.

'What are you going to do with the glass marbles?' Chas asked.

'Ask me stupid questions and you'll be bloody amazed what I'll do with them,' The Irishman said. 'You think I want that stuff slopping around in the bottle? The marbles are to bring the nitro up to just below the stopper. You do it. Roll them in down the neck one at a time. I'll put the tea in – that's a much more skilled operation. And if there's any marbles left over, I'll give you a game before we go out.'

'We?'

'You'll have to show me the place. For fifty quid you can be passing me up the sand.'

In the late evening they went out. Chas insisted on walking a hundred yards ahead. He said that they should not be seen together. In fact, he had no wish to walk in close company with the nitroglycerine. They met up again to buy fish suppers from a shop which was about to close and ate them, loitering in the car park behind the shopping centre while traffic slowed and died and lights went out in the windows. The Irishman gave the last of his fish to a stray cat.

The car park lamps were out but enough light reached them from more remote street lamps for their adjusted eyes to see what they were doing. When The Irishman judged that the town was asleep, they picked their way through the builder's debris to the wall of the shopping centre. He placed his bottle at the bottom of the wall and made his way on to the flat roof by way of a bin-store wall. It was as Chas had described and drawn it. He leaned over the further gutter, lifted the external box of the alarm system off its hooks and laid it on the asphalt of the roof. So far so good. He re-crossed the roof and whispered down to Chas. 'Pass my bottle up and then start filling empty cement bags with sand.'

Very carefully, Chas handed up the bottle and looked for a shovel, failing which he used his hands.

The Irishman placed the bottle on a remote corner of the roof. Somebody might interrupt him and he might have to run for it. He would leave the bottle there. And, he thought grimly, if some damned fool drank out of it and then, as he would, fell down, he would drift across the town as a pale pink mist.

He found the rooflight. It was not an acrylic dome but was built with patent glazing and wired glass. He took out his knife and lifted the lead along the edges until a whole pane was ready to be removed. His friend the cat had followed him up and kept getting in the way, sniffing at his fishy fingers. He gave it a push. 'You bugger off,' he said softly. 'If you're still around when the stupid cops show up, you'll get the blame.'

Chas had filled as many empty cement bags as he could find. The Irishman lay down on his stomach. Standing on a barrow, Chas passed the bags up to him. Sand trickled into his face. The Irishman gave him the empty bags to re-fill. Laboriously, the mound of sand over the alarm box grew higher. The heavy work was exhausting to one in Chas's state of health and his bruised muscles protested until the exercise eased them. The other drove him on, lashing him with whispered words. At last The Irishman was satisfied. He packed the sand down hard and then spoke to Chas for the last time. 'You better get away now,' he said. 'See you later.'

'Good luck,' Chas said. He retreated thankfully.

The Irishman went back to the rooflight. The cat had returned and he shooed it away more forcefully. He lifted out the pane of glass and set it flat on the roof. It was time for a test. He sat down and dangled his legs through the opening. He saw the red eye of one of the sensors come on, and there was a faint, plaintive sound from the pile of sand.

If the alarms were linked to the police station, the police would be along in a minute. He descended into the car park and walked away. He smoked a contemplative cigarette in a dark doorway.

Up on the roof, the cat sniffed at the bottle and gave it a pat with a curious paw. Then, deciding that the bottle held nothing of interest, the cat moved on. Coming to the rooflight it discovered that there was now a way inside where there had never been one before. New places often meant mice, or food left carelessly around. The cat went in, silently, by way of the top of a filing cabinet, and began to explore. The alarm system detected it and made frantic noises under the muffling sand.

When The Irishman returned, there was no sign of the police. He climbed to the roof and fetched his bottle. After prospecting with a pencil torch he leaned in and placed the bottle safely on the filing cabinet, then lowered himself to the full stretch of his arms and dropped. The cat, alarmed by the sudden noise, crouched under the cashier's counter.

The safe was a familiar model. The construction was stout but the hinges and locking-bar were weak. There was only one quick way into it. He took the plasticine from his pocket and opened his knife again. With the back of the blade he packed the plasticine into the joint around the door, forcing it as far back as he could.

When he was sure that the nitroglycerine could not leak inwards into the safe he began again, this time sealing the outer edge. At the top he built out a small cup-shape. When the explosive was poured in, it would flow round all the edges of the door. Then he would place his detonator and fold the plasticine cup over it.

The cat had sensed that there was no danger. It caught the smell of fish and the faint odour of its old friend. It came out from under the counter and moved towards him, pausing to investigate whatever lay in its path.

The Irishman picked up his bottle and then paused. Holding the bottle loosely by the neck, one-handed, he stepped back, intending to take one more look at his workmanship. The escape of a drip could be disastrous.

His foot came down on the cat.

The resulting screech sounded like the end of the world.

For him, it was.

While Chas and The Irishman were lurking behind the shopping centre, 'Uncle' Joe Sulliman arrived in town. He took a taxi to his usual hotel. The porter made haste to bring his cases inside. Uncle was a good tipper when he could see a future return.

Fat Alec arrived an hour later and was taken up to Uncle's room. They spent the first hour on business. When Uncle was satisfied that the pusher's accounting was in order, when he had delivered the fresh consignment and locked the cash away, they were ready to relax.

Uncle poured drinks. 'Any news of The Irishman?' he asked.

Fat Alec shook his head. 'I've been keeping my ear to the ground since you phoned,' he said. 'One of my clients said I'd better speak to Nelson Daw. Then he clammed up. That's all I know.'

Uncle knew Nelson Daw – not as a customer but because, when setting up a team for a major robbery, it was his habit to conclude all arrangements in advance with whichever fence he considered most suitable for the disposal of the expected booty.

'I'll give him a ring in the morning,' he said.

He spent the evening making his own discreet enquiries. He satisfied himself that his man was alive and back on home ground, but without finding any clue to his whereabouts. He slept well, quiet undisturbed by the reverberation from the shopping centre a mile away. In the morning, on the stroke of nine, he phoned the antique shop.

He caught Daw in the act of opening up the shop. The fence took his call in the office. When he realised who was speaking, Daw felt a rare spasm of nerves. Uncle swam with the big fish.

'Sean O'Connell hangs out around these parts, doesn't he?' Uncle said.

'Somebody with a name like that brings me pieces from time to time,' Daw said carefully.

'I used to know him. I'd like to get back in touch.'

Daw thought quickly. If Uncle wanted The Irishman there must be a big job in the offing. There might be more profit in selling The Irishman's services for a smaller percentage of a larger haul. In any case, Uncle was not the right man to disoblige.

'I might be able to help you,' Daw said. 'Perhaps we should meet.'

At his end, Uncle smiled benignly. Daw was right, this was not a subject to discuss on the phone. 'I'll come in and visit you later in the morning,' he said. 'My wife's birthday falls next week. I was thinking of a figurine.'

'I have just the thing,' Daw said. He hung up and looked through his one-way mirror. Chas had just entered the shop with a folded newspaper under his arm.

Daw beckoned Chas into the office. Chas looked less than half-slept.

'You've brought the money?'

'No.'

'Don't tell me that bugger's bolted with it.'

'I don't think so,' Chas said. 'He went in all right. He said I could go. But I just went up the street a bit and waited. He said that it wouldn't make more than a soft thump, but after a bit there was one hell of a bang. The cops were on the scene in one minute flat so I split. But, up to then, he didn't come out. And now, have a look in the local rag, the Stop Press.'

Nelson Daw looked.

> An explosion occurred during the night at the rent office in the Bolder's Green Shopping Centre. It is understood that at least one man died in the explosion. A police spokesman said that the men appeared to have been attempting a robbery but bungled the use of explosives to open the safe. The remains were said to be beyond identification. Other clues to identity are being sought.

Daw's mind turned over the implications. 'You want to buy the girl back?' he asked.

'Would you take twenty quid?'

For a moment Daw was tempted to fix his loss. But then he realised that it wouldn't do. After being loose in his store for a week, Sylvia could not be allowed back on the streets. It was a shame to lay out more money just when he was trying to gather up every penny, but needs must. He had just decided to offer the job to The Irishman when he realised that that convenient disposer was not available any more.

'No, I wouldn't,' he said. 'She'll have to be put down and buried. Want to do the job, for two hundred?'

Chas had once thought that he would do anything for two hundred, but this was more than he could stomach. And Fat Alec had been hinting that The Irishman's services were still in demand. 'Nobody but us knows The Irishman's dead,' he pointed out. 'Is it worth ten per cent if I find you another buyer for the girl?'

Daw remembered Uncle's phone call. 'Nice thinking, Chas,' he said. 'But I'll find my own buyer, thanks very much. You want money, you go and get me some more video recorders. Run along now.'

Chas walked out. He was not happy. Within a week, he was going to be short of money again. He had been sure that there was more money to be made out of the girl. His nerves rebelled at the idea of going back to break-ins. He wondered how he could cash in on the remaining bomb.

Uncle made his appearance shortly before lunchtime. He knew better than to appear eager when dealing with Nelson Daw. The fence had fetched a bottle of Uncle's favourite sherry, and they chatted about generalities for a few minutes before they reached the subject which was on both their minds.

'I could use The Irishman's services,' Uncle said at last. 'I'm told that you might know where he is.'

Daw had decided to commit himself. His plans were so advanced that he could clear the area within a few days.

'He's doing a job for me up north,' he said. 'Contractor's wages.'

'And so the sighting in Glasgow?'

'The police scared him off.'

'I heard he's moved to Liverpool.'

'That's what you were meant to hear.'

'Ah.' Uncle was satisfied. He beamed. 'I have a job for him.'

It was time to give the bait a twitch. 'I can sell him to

you,' Daw said. 'I have him over a barrel. Listen to this.' He played his tape of Sylvia's voice. 'The girl's safely tucked away. Whoever has her can make The Irishman jump through hoops. I promised him this if he did half-a-dozen jobs for me.' Daw showed Uncle the passport. 'And he can do what he likes with the girl.'

'What a cunning old sod you are,' Uncle said admiringly. 'And I suppose he's working for peanuts. How much for the use of him for one job in ten days' time?'

'Forty per cent of the take,' Daw said.

'How much?' Uncle's voice went up to a squeak.

'Have some more sherry.'

Uncle recovered his smooth and smiling manner. 'It's a four-man job,' he said. 'The peterman can't take two-fifths. What'd be left for the rest wouldn't be worth the risk.'

Now it was time to sink the hook. 'He's a wasting asset,' Daw said. 'He could be taken at any time. I've got to cash in my investment while I can.'

Uncle thought quickly. The plan was so big that forty per cent would be a very large sum of money, but he was not going to tell Daw that. 'Perhaps you'd do better to sell out,' he said. 'I've got better contacts for hiding him out between jobs. Would you take fifteen K for the girl and the passport?'

Daw pretended that it was his turn to think. 'Make it twenty,' he said at last.

'Seventeen,' Uncle said.

'Sold to the gent in the black 'at,' Daw said jovially.

They adjourned for lunch.

TWELVE

Sylvia waited, as hours and then days dragged by, for Jimmy to return. But when, once, she heard sounds of his arrival, the reflected daylight lasted only a few seconds and when she got to the bars the oak door was closed again and there was a box of groceries within reach. She uttered an unladylike sound of rage and frustration. She was sure that he had been avoiding her out of shame and that if she could only draw him into calm discussion again she could bring him back under her sway.

For several more hours she bided her time, hiding herself within her books and music. There was even some relief in a passive role. With no more decisions to be taken there was no point in worrying. She slipped back into her former state of apathy.

The sound of another visitation brought her running to the bars. Her heart lifted when she heard a key in the barred gate. When she saw Nelson Daw and two strange men beyond the bars she stopped dead, frozen between hope and fear.

'Do I get to go home now?' she asked.

'Soon,' Daw said gruffly. 'The furniture goes. You stay.' It would not be long before Uncle discovered that The Irishman was dead, and Uncle knew some very hard men indeed. Daw, on the other hand, considered himself to be at the cerebral end of the criminal scale. He had decided to cut and run.

'At least tell me what's happening,' Sylvia begged.

'No questions,' Daw said. He pushed through the barred gate, the two men following.

His curt tone was the final straw to Sylvia's morale. She darted for the doorway. One of the men side-stepped and caught her with one arm round her waist, swinging her round like a child. She started to scream. The man put a hand over her mouth. His fingers smelled of tobacco and other things. She began to choke. She knew that the man was enjoying himself.

'None of that,' Daw said. 'Strangers could come noseying around outside.' He came towards her, feeling in his pocket. Sylvia's head was twisted towards the ceiling and she could only see him out of the corner of her eye. The man took his hand from her mouth and she managed one quick wail before her mouth was taped. A handcuff was snapped on to one of her wrists. It was Nelson Daw's pride that, if a need were foreseeable, he would foresee it. They pushed her back against a thick pipe which ran up the wall, passed the links of the handcuff behind it and clipped her other wrist.

'Start near the door, and take the big stuff first,' Daw said.

The men stripped off dust sheets and began to carry out furniture while Daw began a tour of his Aladdin's cave. Sylvia could do nothing but stand, shaking with fear and guessing at the wrath to come. She had only a partial idea as to the value of the furniture which she had usurped, but she did not expect her nest-building to be approved.

His squawk of horror was enough to confirm her fears. It was repeated, an octave higher, when he found a fragment of the jade figurine which had escaped her broom.

She heard him coming and she had nowhere to flee He stood before her, shaking a fist in front of her face. He found his voice at last. 'You crazy bitch, museums have grovelled for worse stuff. Kings and emperors would find that carpet too fine for their feet, and you've put you grubby little hooves over it. They'd be proud to sit in those chairs and your smelly arse has defiled them. They'd have respected that table, but you've made rings . . . rings on it! And my jade! God, my jade! I could . . . I could . . .' In his fury, he gripped her nose. She tried to jerk her head aside but his hold was too firm. She began to smother. 'It's your good luck that there isn't a thing in here that's not far too valuable to lay across your backside. If I had a riding-crop . . .'

The men watched, grinning. They had been selected for the task because each had been foolish enough to sell Daw evidence which would convict him of a major crime of violence. Their silence was assured. But they could still enjoy the sight of their tormentor's loss of face.

He released her nose. In the moments before she could draw air again, she thought that she was going to pass out. She concentrated on breathing and when her eyes cleared he had gone. He was back in a minute or two with a whippy stick which he had cut from a tree outside. He tucked it through the belt of her dress, gave her a meaningful look and left her again. His intention was clear. Later.

She stood there for hours; how many she could not tell with her watch out of sight. She guessed that there were two vans, because there was a delay and the sound of engines when the first was full. They must have been pantechnicons, from the volume which went out to them. When the men broke for a sandwich lunch one of them, kinder than his mate and less ill-disposed than Daw, untaped her mouth for a minute and gave her a drink of tea. He even helped her to blow her nose.

During the afternoon, the men reached her living corner. They took everything except the food and the camp beds and the few living utensils. When they carried out the furniture, she realised that her clothes, books, tapes, cosmetics, even her toothbrush were going with it. She let them go, rather than attract Daw's attention to herself.

When the basement was empty, they switched the light off and left. Soon, it was clear that Daw was not coming back. She thought that she would have preferred the beating.

Daw had genuinely forgotten Sylvia among his other preoccupations. He was half way to his rendezvous with an innocent pair of replacement drivers for the hired vans when he remembered the girl. He had had no intention of beating her – violence to women was not his line, and he was already ashamed of his outburst. He wondered whether to call in on his way home and release her from the pipe, but decided not to bother. She hardly mattered any more.

Sylvia spent a miserable night, shifting around as much as she could to relieve the creeping stiffness which came over her. Later, a new problem took her mind off her other woes for an hour. She managed at last to relieve herself between her feet and to restore her still dry clothing to decent order. She could never have managed it without the stick.

Jimmy backed the van to a halt outside the ramshackle garage next morning and stopped the engine.

Nelson Daw, in the other front seat, stirred. 'Before we go in,' he said, 'I've something to tell you.'

'Yes, Mr Daw?'

'We've come to the end of the line, you and me, Jimmy. I don't think we've done badly by each other over the years, have we?'

Jimmy shook his head, round-eyed.

'From tomorrow, I'll be a long way off. I've already sold the shop. The sale of this basement back to the pottery goes through today. I had it emptied yesterday, all but the girl and she's also sold. Your last job for me will be to deliver her where she's going. Can you do it without any emotional complications?'

'No problem, Mr Daw.'

'You're a good boy, Jimmy.' He produced an envelope. 'This, by my reckoning, squares us up. You can count it if you like.'

Jimmy pushed it into a pocket. 'No need for that, Mr Daw.'

'You don't get a pension in this sort of work,' Daw said thoughtfully. 'But you can keep the electronics side of the business for yourself if you like. You know the drill as well as I do by now, probably better. You'll need a van. You can have this one for a thousand, which is less than it's worth.'

Jimmy had far more than a thousand in his Giro account, but he had learned a lot from Nelson Daw. 'I couldn't manage a whole grand,' he said. 'Seven hundred's the best I could do. It's more than a garage'd give you unless you was trading it in.'

Daw gave a grunt of irritation. 'I could get twelve if I advertised it,' he said.

'You might, Mr Daw. But you might have to wait for it. I could go to seven-fifty and have cash for you tonight.'

'All right, Jimmy,' Daw said. 'I've taught you too well. You take this . . . ' he handed over a packet containing the passport and the cassette ' . . . and hand it over with the girl at the address I've written on it. You can find it?'

'Easy, Mr Daw.'

'You bring back another packet to me and your own seven-fifty and I'll sign the van over to you. And you can start up with any stock that's in it at the moment. Fair?'

Jimmy nodded.

'Come and get your last consignment of goods.'

Sylvia, drooping in exhaustion against her pipe, heard the door open and saw Jimmy with Mr Daw. She felt a rush of relief. Soon she would be able to stretch and to breathe easily. All night, the tape had resisted her attempts to rub it off against her shoulder.

But when Daw, after one contemptuous glance at the half-dried puddle between her feet, had unlocked one bracelet of the handcuffs and freed it from the pipe he pulled her hands together again behind her back. Sylvia fought, desperately and despairingly, but when Jimmy joined in it was to add his strength to Daw's. She delayed the inevitable for no more than a few seconds. The bracelet clicked and she was fast again.

'Take her outside,' Daw said.

Sylvia tried to sense some promise of help in Jimmy's touch, but his grip on her arm was hard and when they reached the van he pushed her roughly in through the back doors. She fell on her side on the floor mats. Daw followed them out. He gave Jimmy the radio-cassette. 'This is part of your stock,' he said. 'You'd better hand over the rest of the food with the girl. And here's the key to the cuffs. I'll see you tonight.'

'Yes, Mr Daw.'

'There's some cord in the toolbox. You'd better tie her ankles. You won't want her getting up and showing herself.'

She heard Daw get into the Rover and drive off. Jimmy left her alone but closed the back doors and climbed into the front. As the van moved off, she saw trees sliding by overhead.

Surely, she thought, surely Jimmy was going to help her? And after a mile or two of country roads, Jimmy slowed and turned on to a less even surface. He parked with the windscreen almost into some evergreens and climbed between the seats.

She rolled over to offer her wrists for the handcuff key, but he forced her on to her back again. 'This is our last chance,' he said. He took her violently, there on the floor of the van. She was not ready. The experience was pleasureless and even painful, but she was most aware of the handcuffs cutting into her wrists and back.

When he had finished, he fetched the cord and tied her ankles to the frame of one of the front seats. He drove on, singing to himself. Everything was going his way.

THIRTEEN

When, after a few days, Chas found himself out of money and running short of his drug, he faced the fact that he must return to the old, nerve-grinding routine. He reminded himself, as he had often done in the past, that the choice was between the risk of the cold turkey cure if he was caught as against the certainty if he did nothing. He wondered whether to give it all up and sign himself into hospital for the cure but pushed the thought out of his mind. Some day, but not yet.

Chas had his own technique which he brought back into service. He was strictly a day-time operator, preferring to enter empty houses rather than make a silent invasion while the family was asleep or watching television.

He set his old alarm clock, which was only used when he was going out on business. His first need was for transport. He was watching a car park near some shops before dawn and watched the first shopkeeper arrive and park. It was a reasonable bet that the car would not be missed at least until lunchtime. Chas was away with the car before the man had raised his shutters.

Chas drove to the other end of the city and circled until he found an irregular street of expensive houses. He drove through, twice, noting which houses had alarms and which were least overlooked by their neighbours. Then he parked where he could watch the comings and goings. He put on a set of overalls, tucked his hair into a cloth cap and began to change a wheel, spinning out each step and reversing his actions whenever he could be sure that he was not overlooked.

While pretending to work, he watched the pattern developing. Husbands left for work and would be gone for the day. Some wives also drove off, or travelled with their husbands. One even obliged him by carrying her own briefcase. In the other direction, nannies and daily helps arrived. Some of the wives took children with them; they might return or go on to work.

After an hour, he had an accurate picture of which houses were occupied and which were empty, and he had chosen his first target. He left the car where it was and walked. The lady of the house had driven off first. The husband, leaving later, had closed the gates and the doors of the double garage behind him. Unless there were a resident nanny, the house was empty. There was no sign of children, no toys or bicycles, no swing in the garden. He rang the bell at the back door and waited, ready with his story. Nobody came.

There was a sash-and-case window to a downstairs cloakroom. He pulled on a pair of thin gloves, slipped the latch with a knife-blade and was inside with the window closed in the time that it took for a car to pass the house.

He listened, over his own heartbeats, to the silence of an empty house.

He unlocked the back door. There was a clear escape route down the garden if somebody came.

The living room had a picture window overlooked from the street. He would have to empty it on his hands and knees. He studied it through the open door and knew that he had struck gold - a video recorder, a good, slimline television and a complete hi-fi system.

He would need suitcases. He went upstairs and found the master bedroom. There was a bathroom en suite and he used it. These excursions always activated his bowels and bladder. He left it as neat as he had found it.

There was no immediate sign of suitcases. Perhaps

they were in a boxroom. He stooped to check under the bed and saw the wallet, lying half-hidden where it had fallen, presumably from the pocket of a garment in the process of being donned.

He looked inside. There was a fat wad of ten-pound notes, more than enough for his weekly needs.

Chas hesitated. He was reluctant to leave the gold mine downstairs. On the other hand, the wallet would be missed. The man might return at any moment. Chas decided to leave the house locked and tidy without delay. The man would assume that he had lost his wallet elsewhere and Chas could return in a week or two.

At that moment, he heard the front door open and hurried footsteps on the stairs. He backed into the bathroom and pushed the door to. The wallet was in his hand. He shoved it into his pocket and cursed himself. If he had dropped it in the open the man would have taken it and gone and Chas could still have cleaned out the living room. Too late, now. The man would certainly look to see whether he had left it in the bathroom. Chas remembered the man who had left the house – a man who looked both fit and bad-tempered. He looked around. There was a heavy, glass jar of bath essence at the foot of the bath. He lifted it. As the door opened, Chas began his swing.

The jar caught the man on the temple. Perfumed essence sprayed Chas and the small room. The man went down, hitting his head on the toilet bowl as he went.

Chas bent down. A deep gash in the man's temple was oozing no more than a few drops of blood. The body gave him hope by twitching and gasping but then became still. The eyes were open but inert and when Chas touched one of them there was no reaction.

Since his days of unwilling abstinence, Chas had brought forward the time of his fix to the morning. He had taken his day's ration before he left home. His mental agility might not be what it had been the year before, but at least for the moment he was not thinking through treacle.

There was no way to disguise the death as an accident.

If he walked through the streets stinking of a woman's perfume, he would be remembered by a dozen witnesses and connected with the crime.

If he borrowed clothes from the dead man and were caught, they would be conclusive evidence against him.

If he transferred that damning perfume to the car, another mark might register against him.

If he stayed to change his clothes, somebody else might come.

The last was the clincher. He patted his pocket to be sure that the wallet was safe and left the house by the back door.

The garden backed onto a golf course. Chas slipped down between the shrubs, found a gate at the end and let himself out on to a section of rough at the back of a green. The far side of the course bordered on open country. Chas set himself to walk half way round the city on farm tracks without ever coming within ten yards of another person. The onset of rain made the going harder but helped to wash him clean.

Uncle was back in town. He found a message at his hotel and followed it up to meet Fat Alec at the bandstand in the park. They took shelter from a passing shower under its roof. The park was deserted and they could talk freely.

'When's your next appointment?' Uncle asked.

'Two hours' time in the changing room of the public baths.'

'Right. Your message sounded urgent so I came straight away. And you said "meet", not "speak".'

'I didn't see how I could say this on the phone,' Fat Alec said. 'You told me to watch for The Irishman.'

'Is he back?'

'I'm wondering if he went away. I didn't see this until after you'd gone.' Alec produced a page from the local paper. It said little more than had been said in the Stop Press.

Before reading the article, Uncle folded the paper so that no remote watcher could see the headline. 'It's not like The Irishman to make a mistake like that,' he said.

'You only do it once.'

'That's for sure. But he's known for a skilled and careful worker. That's why I wanted his services. What makes you think this is . . . was him?'

'Hunch,' Fat Alec said. 'And Nelson Daw left town suddenly. His shop's empty and I hear they're going to open an Oxfam there.'

Uncle looked considerably less benign than usual. It was not often that he used his own money to set up a caper, but there had been no time to find a backer. He looked again at the page of newsprint and realised that it referred to events during the night before his purchase of the girl. He grew a hunch to match Fat Alec's. He had been conned.

'That customer of yours,' he said. 'The one who said you should speak to Daw. When are you seeing him?'

'Tuesday, eleven o'clock, waiting room at the health centre,' Fat Alec said promptly.

'Too far off. Know where he lives?'

'Just over there.' Alec nodded towards the down-market side of the park.

'Are there any hard men around here now, if The Irishman's gone?'

'If I can do anything . . . ?'

Uncle frowned at him and then shook his head. 'One man, one job,' he said. 'You stick where you're valuable.'

'The town's full of hard men. There's one I used that

time the Pole tried to muscle in. He was good.'

'Get him.'

Chas reached home scared to the verge of panic, hungry, exhausted and still reeking of bath essence.

The last half-mile had been a nightmare of back alleys. Then he had loitered at the edge of the park while he made as sure as he could that the police were not already in wait. He was driven to risk entering at last by the build-up of pedestrians at the end of the working day. He darted up the stairs into the flat and sighed with relief. The lingering perfume on the stairs would be blamed on the lady in the top flat.

He had to go, and quickly. Apart from the possibility that he had been seen, his prints were all over the borrowed car. And they were on record. From whenever the car was found, they would be after him in an hour. By itself, the theft of the car would not be conclusive evidence. In conjunction with the smell of bath essence, or with the money which would probably be traceable to the dead man, it could send him up for murder.

He switched on the immersion heater, and then the radio so that he could monitor any news. He started to prepare a quick meal while the bathwater warmed. When the pans were on the stove, he threw a change of clothing on to the bed, stripped off and bundled the perfumed clothes into a plastic bag for dumping a long way off. He thought that he could save time by eating while he soaked away the smell of his guilt. Then into the clean clothes. A quick meet with Fat Alec and run for it. He felt the tank. Barely warm.

The knock on the door caught him standing, naked and flat-footed, in the kitchen. The shock was so great that his sphincter nearly let him down. He put out his hand to turn down the radio and then decided that that would be a worse giveaway than a radio playing in an empty flat. He waited, quivering.

The knock came again and then a voice. 'Come on, Chas. Open up.'

The voice was familiar but he couldn't place it. He was fairly sure that it was not the police.

'Who is it?' His voice was husky and at the same time squeaked.

'It's me. Alec. Open up.'

He could have fainted with relief. 'Hang on a moment while I get some clothes on. Don't go away.'

'Open up now,' Alec's voice said. 'I'm not shy. If you ever want anything from me again . . . '

That was the Open Sesame. Chas unlocked the door. Three men pushed in. Chas backed into the kitchen and they followed, first an elderly gentleman followed by an obvious bruiser with Fat Alec bringing up the rear and pausing to lock the door behind them.

There were only two, hard chairs in the kitchen. Uncle took one. His usually benevolent face was vicious. Fat Alec moved the other chair against the door and sat down. The bruiser sat on the draining board. Chas was left standing in mid-floor, naked and afraid.

They let him sweat through an ominous silence.

'This place smells like a whore's crotch,' the bruiser said suddenly. 'Is the guy a poof?'

Chas was stung. 'No, I'm not,' he said.

The bruiser reached out a foot and kicked him, right on one of the bruises left by The Irishman. 'You speak when you're spoken to.'

'Is he?' Uncle asked Fat Alec.

'I don't think so,' Alec said. 'It was his bird Nelson Daw sold you, remember?'

Chas understood suddenly and his knees felt weak. He was in more dire trouble. 'Look,' he began.

The bruiser kicked him again, harder.

'Let him speak,' Uncle said. 'I want him to speak. I want him to tell me all he knows about The Irishman. Speak up, little man. Is The Irishman a goner?'

'Yes,' Chas whispered.

'And you were the bright boy who referred Alec to Nelson Daw?'

'He wasn't dead then,' Chas said.

'He was dead when Daw sold the girl to me, which made her valueless. And now Daw's skipped out and taken everything with him.'

'If he's skipped,' Chas said unhappily, 'I didn't know it. Christ, I was out today on the hunt for stuff to take to him!'

'You were, were you? Where is it, then?'

Chas's eyes flicked to the wallet on the table. 'I didn't get anything. It went wrong.'

Uncle took a gold pencil from his pocket and opened the wallet on the table. The pack of banknotes was the brightest thing in the room. There was a printed card behind plastic. 'Ivor Yates,' he read out. 'Holly Tree, Park Crescent. The unfortunate Mr Yates has gone some way towards redeeming my loss.'

'Don't take it all,' Chas said. 'I need some to get away from here.'

The panic in his voice was so evident that all three stared at him. 'Why?' Uncle asked.

'Because I killed him, that's why,' Chas said. 'I didn't mean to. He came back for his wallet and caught me in the bathroom so I belted him with a jar of bath salts or something. That's what the smell is.'

'Very interesting,' Uncle said. He extracted the money, carefully so as not to touch the wallet, and put it in his pocket. 'And very convenient.' He looked at the bruiser and back again at Chas. 'This should just about pay for your disposal. I think a fit of remorse. Head in the gas oven?'

The bruiser nodded. 'And the girl?' he asked. 'She'd be extra.'

Uncle shook his head. 'The girl knows nothing, except about Daw and about this young yob. Who cares about either of them? She can go back to her parents. But you, my young friend, know too much. I hate to lose a good customer, but we must all make sacrifices.'

The bruiser slipped off the draining board and gripped Chas by the elbows from behind. His grip was so strong that Chas felt his own hands begin to tingle and then to go numb. 'You don't have to snuff me,' Chas said desperately. 'I can't talk, with that hanging over me.'

'You'd talk,' Uncle said. 'If the filth took you, you'd tell them anything you knew in the hope of buying an easier deal. Or they'd tempt you with a fix. You junkies are a bad risk. Look in the cupboards,' he told the pusher. 'If you can find some drink, we'll feed him a bellyful and then leave them to it.'

Fat Alec found a bottle of The Irishman's whiskey, still more than half full.

'That should do it,' Uncle said. 'Just what a suicide would take before the deed.'

It had seemed that Chas's mind would never recover in time to work again, but as the bottle approached his face one clear thought came to him. He gabbled it out as quickly as he could spill the words. 'You can still get your investment back,' he said. 'And more. Get me away from here before the police come and I'll show you how.'

FOURTEEN

Sylvia still had no way to measure the passing time, but she guessed that at least two hours had gone by. After a long run on main roads or motorway they had entered streets. Again she was guessing, but from the density of the traffic around them she thought that they were in a major city. She endured the discomfort and clung to hope.

Jimmy stopped to study a street map and then drove on again. They made several turns and left the traffic behind. Another turn and they were on gravel and the van pulled up.

Jimmy got out. Sylvia lifted her head but the windscreen only showed her a blank wall. She could hear his voice, not far away. He came back to the van and reversed in a quarter-circle. The engine stopped. He turned in his seat and untied her ankles from the seat frame but left them joined on a short hobble. He stepped between the seats and over her body, still holding the hobble so that she was dragged round. He opened the back doors and pulled her along the floor of the van.

The van had been backed to within three feet of a house door, so that with both back doors opened she was effectively screened from seeing or being seen. He pulled her roughly out of the van and stood her on her feet. She looked up but could only see a towering wall – a back wall, surely, for who would hang such a tangle of pipes on a front? Then she was pulled through the door and into a passage which smelled of dust. She heard a woman's voice but the place was dark and her eyes were wet.

Jimmy picked her up, not in his arms but over his shoulder, and they descended some wooden stairs into what looked and smelled like an old-fashioned kitchen. A very old man, nodding beside the range, paid them no attention.

The woman opened a door and switched on a light. Jimmy carried her through and dropped her unceremoniously on a bed. It smelled sour, but at least it was soft – softer than anything she could remember. In her exhaustion, she lay on her face and let her mind go. She was only distantly aware of voices and then Jimmy's footsteps diminishing up the stairs.

The woman returned. Sylvia felt hands on her. She was helped to sit up on the side of the bed. The woman took a seat beside her.

'You poor love,' she said. 'You must hurt. Never mind. We'll soon take those things off and get a cup of tea into you. But first, we're going to have a little talk. You've got to understand the rules of the game.'

Doris Knight had quitted a poor but good home forty years before to become a rich man's mistress. That relationship had only lasted a year. Others had followed, but as the charms of youth had faded the relationships had become shorter and the men less rich.

Shortly after her thirty-fifth birthday, she had taken a good look at her life and acknowledged to herself that she was little better than a prostitute. Indeed, slip one more rung down the ladder and she would join that frai sisterhood. An upward move was overdue.

She had some capital put by, mostly in diamonds, fo her lovers had not been ungenerous; but it was no enough. Not nearly enough.

For several years she had joined Uncle in hi journeyings. They had even shared passion for a whil and had formed an attachment which had lasted throug the years. But when the changing economic scene forced Uncle to change the merchandise which he transported, Doris stepped aside. Armaments, she felt, were not ladylike.

She had reviewed her life again and given thought to the future. She had considered setting up as a madam, but the business of brothel-keeping was hedged with dangers. For one thing, while prostitution was legal within certain limits, brothel-keeping was not. For another, it was a competitive field and the competition was not always fair. More often, it was violent.

Studying the problem with cold logic, she realised that she would need a clientèle of the rich and powerful. Therefore she must provide a service which attracted such a clientèle. Her considerable experience provided the next step in her reasoning. Rich and powerful men came, in the main, from that class of society whose upbringing and schooling fitted them admirably for every field of endeavour except for sex. If she were to provide, very expensively, the facilities which lay beyond the line which a wife would draw, the right sort of clientèle would follow.

London, Paris and other capitals were already well provided with such establishments. But rich men with local clout were not confined to capital cities. Helped by Uncle, whose knowledge of esoteric geography already outstripped any gazetteer, she found an untapped area rich with the clients of her choice, and established herself in a former vicarage. Although Sylvia could not know it, he building above their heads was furnished in the height of luxury.

Business had been good. A select but eccentric ross-section of the world had beaten a path to her door nd she had soon compiled a list of ladies one or another f whom would, for cash or under duress, indulge a isitor in almost any game which his ingenuity might envisage.

It had been a good life but the permissive society was killing it.

'So what's the inspiration?' Uncle asked grimly. 'It had better be good. A suicide by exhaust fumes would be just as convincing.'

They were sitting in Fat Alec's van inside the lock-up garage which he rented under a fictitious name. Alec never drove and the van's engine had not turned over in years, but only he knew that and it seemed an inappropriate time to mention it. The van was his repository for cash and for his stock of drugs.

Chas was on the bench front seat, jammed between Fat Alec and the bruiser. He had to speak awkwardly over his shoulder to Uncle who was at ease on a plush-upholstered armchair in the back. Alec often spent long hours in the van between appointments.

'You've already got the girl,' Chas said. 'Her parents are well heeled. Ransom her.'

'How well heeled?'

'A valuable house, and I know it's not mortgaged because he was talking taxation when I was there. Twenty thousand a year job, maybe a bit more. Some investments.'

'So his borrowing capacity is high,' Uncle said. 'Come to the crunch figure. How far would he go for his daughter before he'd decide that the figure was too high and that he'd rather leave it to the police and hope for the best?'

'Fifty K would be safe,' Chas said. 'His wife would push him that far. She'd never hold her head up again if it was said that they'd been too mean to ransom their daughter.'

Uncle nodded unseen in the darkness. 'I've never gone in for kidnapping,' he said. 'It's dirty.'

'Then sell her on again,' Chas said. The danger of death seemed to have receded and his devious mind was at work again. He was almost enjoying himself. Chas felt that he would have been at home in the world of big business. 'How much of the work and risk goes into the actual snatch? A third? You could ask fifteen or twenty grand.'

'Half,' the bruiser said. 'Me and some mates could take it on and cut you in for half.'

'Could you put my end down in advance?'

Silence answered him.

'So,' Uncle said, 'if you get taken, I'm still out my investment. And if you pull it off I'm in for half – if your mates don't decide to run off with the lot. The odds don't sound good. I've got a better idea.

'I know somebody who'll do it for nothing.' He prodded Chas in the back of the neck. 'You. And you can't cross me because, as a junkie, you've got to come up for breath now and again in places where I can find you. You'd never be sure that your next fix wasn't loaded with strychnine. If you failed to show up, I'd only have to check around the admission hospitals.

'Listen carefully. You've met the family. You go to them with a tape of the girl's voice carrying the whole message. You explain that, because you're her boyfriend and know her family, you've been approached and sent to act as a go-between. They give you the money to take to the kidnappers, and ten minutes later you come back with the bird. I'll spell out the details for you if you want.'

Chas knew that he had talked himself into something which he did not much like, but there seemed to be no escape. 'Don't I get anything out of it?' he said. 'I've got to go on the run. I need a start.'

'You get your life out of it,' Uncle pointed out. 'That's more than I thought you were going to get away with half an hour ago. After you've done this job I'll return the money that was in the wallet. It looks like about four hundred. That's fair, isn't it?'

'It looks as if it's the best I can do,' Chas said.

Doris Knight – although Sylvia never knew that that was her name – later impressed her captive as being a kind and gregarious person, ladylike in the manner of those who have come up in the world and wish it thought that they have never been anywhere else. She wore real jewellery and too much of it; and Sylvia never saw her other than dressed, coiffeured and made-up as if for an important party. Her accent erred on the far side of Oxford from her humbler beginnings.

Doris seemed pleased to have a 'lodger'. Several times she visited Sylvia with cups of tea, first carefully and apologetically attaching her to the bedhead with the same handcuffs. Then she would seat herself, with a creak of expensive corsetry, in the only chair and chat comfortably for an hour or more. Her favourite topic was the foibles of her dwindling band of clients, but she always discussed them with sympathy. 'They were brought up,' she said once, 'to believe in hellfire, that sex is wicked and that nice women don't. How can you blame the poor old sods if they want to punish or be punished, or to rape or be raped? It's better they do it here than out on the streets.'

She need never have bothered with the handcuffs. Sylvia was far too scared to attempt escape. On that first day, while Sylvia was still cuffed and hobbled and taped, Doris had revealed her other side, the virago who had clawed her way from a working-class beginning to a place in the upper echelons of a tough business. Her revelations had been made more shocking by the contrast of her sweet and gentle voice. She had explained, in terms blunt even for her background, the nature of her business, and she had gone on to mention a gentleman by the name of Willis. Mr Willis was the bogeyman. His desires were such that none of the girls would accept his custom any more. 'He doesn't mean it,' Doris said, 'but when he's got the girl tied up – much the way you are now – and a riding-crop in his hand he gets carried away. He'd pay anything, but money isn't enough, is it? I dare say he'd go to five hundred for a weekend with an unspoiled chit like you, or ten thousand to have you for keeps. I'm supposed to keep you safe, but if you annoy me, love, I'll take the money and to hell with them.'

Sylvia had no way of knowing whether or not Mr Willis existed, nor had she any intention of finding out.

If Doris knew anything about Sylvia's destiny, that was the one subject about which she was not prepared to chatter. If Sylvia asked, Doris changed the subject. And Sylvia quickly sank back into her previous dull state. She was housed and fed. She was safe for the moment in her cubicle. She was even allowed limited and supervised laundry facilities in the kitchen. If that life went on for ever, at least it would be survival.

On Sylvia's third day in Doris's care, the door was suddenly unlocked. 'You've a visitor,' Doris said. 'I'll have to lock you in, but you won't mind that.'

Chas appeared in the doorway. For an instant Sylvia hesitated. Her instincts were suspicious of any change. Then she jumped up and threw herself at his chest. Chas had been wondering what interpretation she had put on his behaviour and prepared to defend himself. But her intentions were not hostile. Her hug, although almost painful, was a mark of affection and relief.

'Chas,' she said. 'Chas, have you come to take me home?'

'Not yet,' Chas said. He gave her a familiar pat and pulled her down with him to sit side-by-side on the bed.

'Oh.' She studied him. 'You've had your hair cut. And new clothes. You look much nicer.'

'Coming to see you . . . ' Chas said. He had also shaved with great care. If his picture or description were circulated, he preferred to be as unlike his previous self as possible. 'You've done something different with your hair,' he added. Girls expected these changes to be noticed.

There were more pressing matters on Sylvia's mind. 'Chas, what's happening?'

'Trouble, I'm afraid. Can you be brave?'

'I think so,' Sylvia said without conviction. 'What trouble?'

'I didn't know anything about it until today,' Chas said, 'but Nelson Daw sold you to a gang who were using you as a threat to make The Irishman do what they wanted.'

'Chas, that's terrible.' It was shock rather than surprise in Sylvia's voice – shock at having her vague suspicions confirmed.

'There's worse to come. The Irishman's dead.'

'Is that really worse? Can't I go home now?'

'You've cost them money.' Chas punched home the words. 'Now there's no Irishman to hold you over as a threat. They were going to kill you. But they can get their money back by ransoming you to your parents.'

'I see.' Hope, which had dried like a seed in the desert, began to grow again.

'They've picked me to act as a go-between,' Chas said. 'I've got a cassette recorder outside. They want you to read this message into it, so that your parents know that you're alive.'

Sylvia studied the words on the paper and looked up. 'Do we have to go through this?' she asked. 'Couldn't you just get me away now? There's only the woman and the old man here. I've been listening to the footsteps.'

'Afraid not,' Chas said. 'I was brought here under guard by two toughs. They're waiting outside the house.'

'But you know where we are. You could go to the police.'

Chas hesitated. 'I don't know where we are,' he said. 'I was blindfolded.'

Sylvia pulled her hands away. She got up and moved to the armchair. 'What are you getting out of it?' she asked in a very small voice.

'Nothing,' Chas almost shouted. 'I told you, I've been picked as a go-between. I'm trying to save you. And I'm under threat myself.'

'Very well, I'll read the message.'

'Good. Put as much fear as you can into it. That ought to be easy,' Chas added viciously, 'because if they don't buy it you're dead.'

After he was gone, Sylvia lay down on the bed and began to shake. She wondered whether she would part with the savings of a lifetime for the sake of a daughter who had treated her with the contempt and derision which she had shown her parents. She thought probably not. But then, she could not imagine the ties of parenthood. Please God they would be strong enough. She prayed for forgiveness, not of God but of her parents.

FIFTEEN

With their respective homes only a few doors apart, Sylvia's friend Rosie could hardly conceal from the Cantor household her unaccompanied return. She tried at first to minimise her own part in the deception by a vague assertion that Sylvia had quarrelled with her and gone her own way and no doubt would be home soon. Cross-examination by both sets of parents had soon established that the separation had been planned and that Rosie, having posted a succession of cards which Sylvia had obtained and written in advance, had been part of the conspiracy.

Mrs Cantor had professed to be alarmed as well as understandably upset. Her frequently expressed doubts as to what Sylvia could be Up To at last exasperated her husband into saying that they knew perfectly well what she was Up To, the only questions in doubt being with whom, where and for how long.

Rather than accept the unacceptable, Mrs Cantor had, over the next few days, driven her mate to distraction by producing a series of ever more improbable theories aimed at providing innocent explanations for Sylvia's behaviour. Mr Cantor, who would have preferred to admit his daughter's sins in order to enjoy her absence, took to reading the newspaper in the locked bathroom and to long walks on the common.

Downright explosion was averted by the arrival of Chas. Sylvia's mother took him into the living room which was both spacious and expensively furnished, making up in luxury what it might have lacked in taste.

'My husband went out for a walk,' Mrs Cantor said. She looked curiously at the cassette recorder which Chas held in his lap. 'Can I help?' she asked.

'I was hoping to see both of you,' Chas said. He fought back a yawn. He seemed to be tired to yawning point more often than not these days.

On the two previous occasions when she had, reluctantly, set eyes on Chas, he had been stubbled, long-haired and dressed in jeans and a leather jacket. The new Chas might have been a stranger. But there was something about him which brought her daughter back to her mind. 'Is it about Sylvia?' she asked hopefully. 'How is she?'

'She's quite well,' Chas said. Further than that he was not going to go until Mr Cantor was present. The woman was quite capable of fainting into his arms or something.

He was saved from all but a minute or so of frantic inquisition by the return of Mr Cantor. Sylvia's father might be, to Chas's eyes, an ageing product of privilege, but he was no fool; and unlike his wife, who noticed hair and clothes, he looked into faces.

'I've seen you with Sylvia,' he said. His eyes narrowed. 'Did she go off with you?'

'She spent a weekend at my flat,' Chas said cautiously.

Mrs Cantor uttered a faint shriek. 'She told us lies,' she complained in her normal voice.

'I don't know what she told you,' Chas said. 'She was only with me for two nights and I slept on the settee.' He thought that the Cantors were more likely to cough up for a virtuous daughter than for the real Sylvia. 'After that, she went off. She said that she wanted some time on her own, to decide what to do with her life without anyone breathing down her neck.'

'Then where is she now?' Mrs Cantor asked.

'That's why I'm here. And, believe me, I'm not

enjoying myself. The next I heard of her was yesterday. A man stopped me in the park and gave me this.'

He played the cassette. Sylvia's voice came over clearly, so clearly that her distress was unmistakable. 'Mummy, Daddy. I'm sorry about this, you won't believe how sorry. I've been kidnapped. They want fifty thousand pounds to let me go. I know it's an awful lot of money, but they say that if it isn't paid I'll be killed and you'll never even know where I'm buried. And,' the voice faltered, 'I believe that it's true. You're being watched, and if the police are called in they'll know and I'll be killed anyway. Chas will bring you this message and he's to act as go-between. I shan't have a chance to speak to you again, so I'm saying please, please, if you can possibly raise the money, please get me out of here. I'm not being ill-treated at the moment.' There was a pause on the tape and then her voice burst out again. 'But I want to live and make it all up to you.'

The tape went silent. Chas shut it off. 'I'll leave you to discuss it,' he said. 'I can't tell you any more. I'll phone you when I get my instructions. And I've got orders to take the cassette away with me.'

Mrs Cantor moaned and fell against her husband's shoulder. Chas made his escape while that gentleman had his hands full.

One hour later, Mrs Cantor, with a large brandy inside her and a cup of strong, sweet tea within reach, was prone on the sofa. Her sobs and shudders were still alternating with a regularity which set her husband's nerves jangling, but they had subsided to the point where she could talk above them.

Her husband, who had recovered from the first shock and was trying to think, hovered over her in case of a relapse.

'The money must be paid,' she said.

'Yes, of course,' Mr Cantor said irritably. As the one who would have to pay it, the decision had been his to take. It would mean postponing his retirement and reducing their standard of living. He wondered who would be the first to complain at that. 'There was never any doubt about it.'

'And no police.'

'That needs thinking about.'

'But you heard what she said!'

Mr Cantor sighed. At the height of her hysterics he had slapped his wife's face. He rather wished that he had the excuse to do it again. 'They were bound to make her say that,' he pointed out. 'But there have been cases when the money was paid but the victim knew too much and wasn't returned. No gang of kidnappers has the resources to watch us all the time.'

'Not the police,' she repeated.

'I'm not handing over every penny we can raise on the strength of a tape recording. Not without getting some expert advice first.'

'What about Mr Meldrum?'

Mr Meldrum was their solicitor, a fragile and dusty man who seemed to belong under a glass dome. 'He'd only go looking for a court order,' Mr Cantor said. He took a turn around the room. 'I don't trust that young man. You didn't either.'

'He looked more presentable than most of the young men she's brought here,' Mrs Cantor said timidly.

'Last time he came, you said you wouldn't trust him alone with your mother.'

'Was that the same one? I thought I'd seen him before.'

'Of course it was the same one,' Mr Cantor said. 'He's cleaned himself up and he wasn't speaking like an out-of-date hippie this time, but that's all that's changed. He's still the same tearaway. I wouldn't be surprised if he had a hand in this.'

'Do you think . . . ?' Mrs Cantor bit the words off.

'What?'

'I was wondering,' she said faintly, 'whether he mightn't have got together with Sylvia and they cooked this up together. Perhaps they wanted money to get married.'

'To start a commune, more likely. Shut up a minute while I think.' He paced slowly around the room. His wife was happy to close her eyes. She had never been at ease with rational thought, her thinking having been done for her by her father and later by her husband.

Mr Cantor had been closer to his daughter than had her mother, but he was quite prepared to consider the possibility that she was involved in a scheme to extort money from her own family. After a full minute, he shook his head. 'I don't think so. The amount was wrong. And she'd have tried to borrow the money off me quite openly first. She wouldn't have got it, but she was never shy of asking. Also, her voice on that tape . . . it sounded like real fear. She was never that much of an actress.'

His wife opened her eyes. 'She was a little madam.'

'But you knew it. She never could hide anything for long. We'll bear the possibility in mind, but I think this thing's real. I just wish I knew somebody who could tell me what I should do,' he finished miserably.

'What about that young man she brought home once? The army officer?'

Mr Cantor knew that the suggestion stemmed from no more than the fact that the captain had been clean and smart. The fact that the idea was also inspired was no more than coincidence. The two men had talked for some time while waiting for the return home of Sylvia, who had quite forgotten her date. At first, the young officer had seemed to be no more than the typical chinless wonder, banished into the army for lack of any mor worthy calling. But, as they talked, Mr Cantor had sensed something both sharper and harder, hidden like a knife blade in butter. He learned that Captain Craythorne had served in Ireland, but on that subject alone he refused to be drawn. It was a friend with military connections who let slip that the captain had been decorated for his courage in going undercover and penetrating one of the most dangerously activist wings of the IRA. Mr Cantor brightened. An experienced anti-terrorist, and one of Sylvia's beaux, would make a better ally than any policeman.

'That might be an idea,' he said. 'What was his name? Crawley?'

'Craythorne. But, now that I come to think of it, he'd be back in Ireland by now.'

'There's been time for him to do another tour and be home again. Anyway, I'll phone the barracks. It doesn't cost much to find out.'

'What if you can't reach him?' Mrs Cantor asked anxiously.

'Then I'll have to speak to the police.'

'No police,' Mrs Cantor said. She went off into the vapours again.

Jonathan Craythorne might have lived out his career as one of a host of competent but undistinguished officers and without ever discovering that he had the sort of stubborn conviction which is the father of true courage, but for two circumstances.

The first of these was that, coming of a nomadic military family, he spent most of his school holidays with an aunt in County Down. There he learned a great deal of Irish folklore and the geography of the province and he developed a brogue which he could drop back into whenever he so wished.

The second circumstance was that he had for a time grown taller and skinnier than his contemporaries at the notable public school where he had spent his youth. This peculiarity had invited the attention of the bullies which are present in even the most modern and best regulated of schools. He went on to Sandhurst with a deep hatred of all who seek to impose their will on others by violence. He had also adopted the protective mannerisms of his class, mastering a style of self-effacement that had persisted long after he had broadened out more than enough to look after himself. Like Fat Alec, he had found that strength is stronger when hidden.

Passing out of Sandhurst among the top ten, he had joined his regiment. His men had thought him soft . . . for about a day. Within a month, any one of them would have followed him anywhere.

The regiment took its turn policing the streets of Belfast. But, before his face had time to become known, he was taken off normal duties. There was call for an officer with a convincing accent and local knowledge. After intensive further training he had been put down the hole like a ferret.

For several months his life had depended on his quick wit and ready tongue. Those months did nothing to lessen his loathing of the terrorist mentality. At the end of that time, more than thirty rabbits had been netted. They had included two visiting Americans in search of kicks on the 'Terrorist Tour', a Catholic priest rash enough to practise what he had secretly been preaching and four of the most dangerous men on the wanted list In the process, his cover had been blown. He wa withdrawn from Ireland and warned never to return.

At the time of Mr Cantor's call, he was reluctantl preparing to go on leave to a cousin who farmed in one c the shires. There he would be expected to shoc partridges. He disliked shooting partridges. Their face reminded him of one of his aunts. He would rather have shot terrorists, who were better for their going and, being able to shoot back, provided better sport.

He took the call in the adjutant's office. 'Is that Captain Craythorne?' asked a vaguely familiar voice.

'It was. Major since last June, actually,' he said.

'Major Craythorne. Steven Cantor here. My daughter invited you to our house about a year ago.'

In Belfast, the major's life had depended on his being alert to the nuances of intonation. There was hidden anxiety in his caller's voice. A minuscule hesitation before the word 'daughter' pinpointed the subject of the anxiety. He felt little surprise. If he ever fathered a daughter with Sylvia's amorality and half her charm, he would worry too. He felt a stirring of interest. Something was coming. But he kept his voice cool and social.

'I remember. How is Sylvia?'

'I . . . need some advice which I think you may be able to give me.'

'I'll call you back in a few minutes.' He broke the connection. 'You don't want me for anything else, James?'

'I never want you,' the adjutant said. 'I just feel mpelled to take you to task when your paperwork falls nore than a year behind. Go and attend to your love fe.'

In the officers' mess, the major found a telephone hich was less vulnerable to eavesdropping. He pro- uced a leather-bound notebook and looked up Sylvia's umber. The names in the notebook were mostly female, nd they were annotated with small symbols. His aperwork was not always as casual as the adjutant had nplied. The symbols against Sylvia's name reminded m that she had gained top marks for charm, appear- nce and for her behaviour in the best hotel room which had been able to command at short notice. It was an acquaintanceship which he would have pursued further but for his posting to Ireland.

Mr Cantor answered the phone at the first ring.

'Tell me what the trouble is,' said the major.

'Sylvia's been kidnapped.'

'Tell me all you can.'

Sylvia's father was accustomed to the making of clear reports. Within a few minutes and after asking only one question the major was in possession of all the salient facts.

'You've dealt with these sort of people before,' Mr Cantor finished. 'I'd value your advice as to whether I should call in the police.'

'Not yet,' the major said. 'Give me time to see what I can find out. Get the money together as soon as you can, but if young Gowans phones again, tell him that you need more time to raise that much in cash. I'll meet you for lunch in The Royal George tomorrow. Even if you're being watched, which is unlikely, you can still meet a friend for lunch.'

'Thank you.' Over the phone, he heard Mr Cantor sigh. 'You don't know what a relief it is . . . '

'I can imagine. My regards to your wife and try not to let her worry too much. I'll see you tomorrow.'

The major sat looking at the dead telephone. Which o his brother officers had been talking about a relative hig up in the local police?

Major Craythorne had chosen The Royal George for hi meeting with Mr Cantor because the dining room of tha hotel, being both expensive and old-fashioned, tended t attract a class of diner among whom the averag criminal, at that level in the pecking order which ge detailed for surveillance work, would have stood out lik a bride at a funeral. Even so, when they took their plac in the corner, he looked hard at the occupants of th neighbouring tables.

He could have spared his eyes. Even if the innocent businessmen discussing the price of microchips or the couple celebrating their ruby wedding had been curious, they could not have overheard a word. A long table down the middle of the room had been booked for a party of ladies who seemed to be old schoolfriends holding their first re-union after many years and therefore, as ladies will, talking shrilly and simultaneously, each raising her voice to try to be heard above all the others.

'I've been in touch with the chief superintendent.' Craythorne had expected to whisper the news. He found that he had almost to shout it.

'Did you tell him about the kidnapping?' Mr Cantor looked older than Craythorne had remembered him, and very tired.

'No. I said that I was making tactful enquiries because you'd lost touch with your daughter and were worried about the company she'd been getting into. When I nentioned the name of Charles Gowans, known as Chas, ne nearly went through the ceiling. Did you know that hat young man was on hard drugs?'

'We suspected it. Something about his eyes.'

'Does Sylvia . . . ?'

'We think not. Perhaps the occasional puff of pot, but hey all do that nowadays. She came to Spain with us hree months ago and wore a bikini which shocked her nother speechless. I thought she looked rather nice,' Mr Cantor added reflectively. 'If she had had any needle narks, the whole of the Costa Brava would have seen nem. And we kept an eye on her possessions while she as at home.'

Major Craythorne breathed a sigh of relief but he ould not pretend to be happy. 'Gowans seems to have een supporting his expensive habit by housebreaking,' said. 'The police have suspected it for some time but never caught him. Now they think that a householder came home unexpectedly and Gowans turned violent. His modus operandi was written all over it and there was a stolen car with his fingerprints in it found not far away. They want to question him.'

Mr Cantor pushed his plate away. His steak was only half-eaten. 'That's bad,' he said.

'Very. The chief superintendent wanted to send men to your house immediately, to dig for any possible clues to Gowans' whereabouts. I had to explain, very firmly, that you had lost touch with your daughter a month ago, that your wife was prostrated with worry, that you couldn't tell them anything and would be grateful not to be bothered by the police until further notice. I promised that you'd get in touch if you heard from Sylvia or from Gowans.'

'Was he satisfied?'

'He seemed so, but he has to pass the word along and he couldn't promise for the officers dealing with the other case. I think I've bought us a few days, which should be enough.'

'Please God! That other case, was it murder? You can tell me,' Mr Cantor said.

'I'm afraid so. That decided me not to mention the kidnapping. When the police have a major case to solve, that becomes top priority. The safety of a kidnap victim may only rank as equal top or even a close second. Our objectives, I take it, are first a safe recovery of Sylvia followed a long way behind by recovery of the money and justice for the kidnappers, in that order. You agree?'

'Definitely,' Mr Cantor said.

'Did Gowans phone?'

'Last night. I asked for another two days to get the money ready. He'll phone again tomorrow evening.'

'That's good timing,' the major said. 'It gives me chance to make my own arrangements and then come t you. Could you have me for a houseguest for a few days?'

'Of course,' Mr Cantor said. He looked fondly at the major who, in a civilian suit of excellent cut and cloth, exemplified the perfect son-in-law. 'She isn't a bad girl, you know.'

The major smiled. 'I do know that,' he said. 'And now I think I'll go. I've things to do. And I'm getting a headache from the din.'

Mr Cantor found that he could smile in return. 'I think I'll brave the din and have some cheese,' he said. 'You've given me fresh hope and I don't remember when I last ate.'

Major Craythorne returned to barracks, changed into uniform and went in search of CSM Heather.

Eric Heather ('Old Tautology' the CO had once called him, but the joke had been over the men's heads) had never known life outside the army. His father had been a famous RSM and Eric had travelled the world with his parents until enlisted as a boy soldier. The life had suited him. When he became the youngest warrant officer in the British Army it had seemed to be no more than his destiny. More than one CO had offered to put him forward for officer training but he had declined. He had no great liking for officers, with one exception. He had been Jonathan Craythorne's sergeant in the Falklands nd each had been surprised to find the other as tough nd professional as himself.

The sergeant-major was at work in his own small ffice. He rose and snapped to attention. He would have one as much for any set of pips or crowns, but in this se the mark of respect was for the man.

'Be seated, sar'nt-major,' Craythorne said. He laid a ll of paper on the desk, took the spare chair and oduced cigarettes. 'Have a smoke. I'm looking for me friendly assistance.'

Heather tidied his own papers and then looked at the other with interest. It was not like the major to want help. 'Go on, sir,' he said.

'My best girl's been kidnapped,' Craythorne said. He was exaggerating Sylvia's status for the sake of sympathy – or, he wondered, was he? The sergeant-major heard him out in silence as he outlined the facts. 'Now,' he finished, 'what strikes you?'

The sergeant-major scratched his short haircut. Fatherly guidance to young officers – who were frequently older than himself – was often his duty, but the major was a different animal. 'You think we'd better handle this ourselves, sir?' he asked. 'No police?'

'Correct. The police have the newspapers breathing down their necks. I think they might be a little too concerned with not letting a murderer slip through their net to lie doggo until the girl's safe. Also, news leaks out of the cop shops; and once a kidnapping gets to be public knowledge, the victim's chances are pretty thin.'

'Just my own thoughts,' the CSM said. 'You realise, sir, the police'll be a bit umpty with us if we leave them out in the cold?'

'They will if we let this man get away. If we call them the minute the girl's safe and deliver Gowans into their hands they won't be in much of a position to complain. But, frankly, I don't care much whether or not we tread on their beastly toes as long as the girl's safe. If we can pull that off, I'll carry the can. Anyone else can fade quietly away.'

'I don't think it'll come to that, sir.' The sergeant-major thought some more. He also had served in Belfast and had learned to think in parallel with terrorists. 'It'll be dodgy. If this bloke Gowans is already on the run for murder, he may be ready to kill again. And God knows what else the girl may be able to shop him for. He may not mean to hand her over alive.'

'That's what I'm afraid of, although I've tried not to let her parents see it that way. And that's also why I'm going to be staying in the house from tomorrow. I'll do the negotiating, and I'll make damn sure they realise that there won't be a sniff of the money until the girl's out in the open.

'I'd like you in control of an outside party. Think you could get about half-a-dozen volunteers? We want hard cases who can handle themselves in the dark – I think this'll come to a head in hours of darkness, don't you? We want chaps who can stick to a plan but bright enough to vary the plan on their own initiative if the need arises.'

'No problem at all,' the sergeant-major said.

'Jolly good show!' said Craythorne with a brief return to his chosen public image. Next moment he was the hard-eyed soldier again. He rolled out his plan. 'Ordnance Survey,' he said. 'Let's consider all the options. Then we'll have a better idea of what manpower and equipment we need.'

SIXTEEN

Jonathan Craythorne entered the Cantor home the following day by the back door. Night had already fallen but an exhaustive reconnaissance in the dusk had assured him that the house was not being watched. Even so, he had approached through the shrubberies of a row of gardens. He dropped his haversack in the hall with some relief – it was heavy with equipment and clothing to suit every variation of plan.

'Anything yet?' he asked.

Mr Cantor shook his head.

'Good. Let's prepare for him before we do anything else. Where's the phone?'

'We can use the one in the living room.'

The major lugged his haversack into the living room. The curtains, he noted, were tightly drawn. He produced a small tape recorder which he attached to the phone. Beside it he placed a personal radio. 'So far so good,' he said. 'You have the money?'

'Under the bed,' Mr Cantor said. He laughed nervously. 'The traditional place. I've been scared to leave the house. And my bank manager thinks I'm being blackmailed.'

'Don't worry about the money. Neither of us is going out again until this is over. As far as your office is concerned, you're ill. Where's your wife?'

'Preparing a meal. I've thought it best to keep her busy.'

'Much the best,' Craythorne agreed. 'Let's pay her a visit. Does your kitchen have curtains? I don't mind being heard but I'd rather not be seen yet, just in case I want to change roles.'

'There's a venetian blind. Give me a start of a few seconds.'

Sylvia's mother had been working in a daze and the intrusion of one of her daughter's man-friends, although by far the best of the bunch, was enough to discompose her altogether. But the major was so charming in his ineffectual, Hooray-Henry way, complimenting her on her lovely house and fetching her a medium sherry, that she soon stopped wondering whether he could possibly help and even giggled at one or two of his little jokes. And he stayed in the kitchen to help her after her husband had retired to the living room, which was absolutely unknown for one of Sylvia's young men. If you could call them men . . .

The dining room was the leg of the L-shaped living room. They sat down to a dinner which was, in the circumstances, remarkably good. The major kept their minds occupied with a succession of military anecdotes. They mostly presented himself in his silly-ass guise, but Mr Cantor was not fooled.

The telephone rang while they were at the cheese. Mrs Cantor spilled her wine glass. The major got up without hurrying and strolled to the phone. He started the tape before he picked up the receiver.

He heard the rapid pips of a coin-operated phone. Money dropped. 'Mr Cantor?' said a voice.

'I'm dreadfully sorry,' said the major, 'but Mr Cantor's ill. Can I take a message?' He had added a lisp to his voice. He wondered whether he wasn't overdoing it.

There was a long pause on the line. Major Craythorne winked at his companions. 'What's wrong with him?' asked the voice.

'Nervous prostration. Can I help?'

'Who are you?'

'Name's Craythorne. I'm a friend of the family. What did you want with Mr Cantor?'

'I wanted to speak to him about his daughter,' Chas said.

'If you're the chap about this kidnapping business,' said the major, 'Mr Cantor's asked me to deal with it. The money'll be here tomorrow afternoon, so we could make an exchange tomorrow evening. But I'm not to hand over the money under any circumstances except in exchange for Miss Cantor alive and well.'

'But that's my job,' Chas said plaintively. 'I was going to make sure she was all right before giving up the money. I don't know that they'll deal on any other terms.'

'Can't help that, old chap. Those are my orders. Sorry, and all that.'

'Don't they trust me?'

'If you were them, would you trust you?'

'I'll phone tomorrow.' The connection was broken.

The major played the tape over the radio to the sergeant-major.

Chas came out of the call box and hurried through the dark side-streets, fuming. He was within a few hundred yards of Sylvia. Uncle had whisked him out of the immediate danger area and had found him the use of a room in a crumbling house occupied by squatters. It was cold and squalid but at least nobody bothered him.

He was furious, but mostly with himself. He had intended to stay cool and to dominate the discussion Instead, he had allowed the initiative to be wrestle away from him, and by a man who sounded like a prope chinless wonder, the type Chas hated above all else. Th ranks of privilege were closing in on him again.

And now his plan was back in the melting pot. He ha

had no intention of returning Sylvia alive. The bruiser was to accompany him, but only to guard Sylvia in the van or car while Chas collected the money. Somewhere between the vehicle and the house he could have managed a quick knock on the head. By the time the deed was discovered he would have been out of the country with the promised passport.

Chas's mind, never very stable, undermined by drugs and now stunned with fear, was too confused to see that his killing of Ivor Yates had put him into much more imminent danger; but his fear that Sylvia could implicate him in the carrying of the bombs to London had had more time to take root. The girl must die.

But how? Chas shrank from violence. He might have nerved himself to destroy a helpless girl, but to fight somebody who might fight back was beyond him.

In the privacy of his miserable room he stretched out on the mattress and thought some more. It was imperative that he got the money. He would not get the money until he delivered the girl. Once she was with her family, she was safe from him. Or was she?

Chas remembered the bomb, and he smiled a smile which wormed its way right through him. He lay in the dark, polishing his design and waiting for the time to steal a car.

For the first time, Doris had left the key in the outside of the door.

For much of the afternoon, sounds of activity had filtered through the door from the kitchen and, when she had last visited Sylvia, the procuress had been dressed and jewelled with even more care and splendour than usual and her manner had been hurried and distant. Other matters were on her mind.

Sylvia thought, on balance, that her parents would probably ransom her. But, once she had recovered from the shock of Chas's visit and set her mind to work, she could hardly have failed to realise that she was in grave danger. Kidnap victims were not always returned alive after the ransom was paid. Please God that those cases were only the newsworthy minority. Her mother might blind herself to the danger, but her father would certainly see it.

Chas, she now knew, was looking out for himself. But her parents might trust him. If her father went to the police, Chas might find out. And then . . .

She had made up her mind to escape if she could, but it was impossible to make a plan. The room was windowless, depending for its ventilation on a wide gap under the door, and her view of the outside world was limited to a segment of the kitchen, seen through the large keyhole, usually featuring the same old man dozing peacefully in his chair. She had opened out a thin, gold bangle which had somehow remained on her arm during her travels and with this poor substitute for a skeleton key she had tried in vain to pick the lock; after which she had sunk again into dull resignation.

With the key in the door, hope woke again. The novels of her teens had told her what to do. She had no newspaper to slide under the door, but there was ample space for the mat which was the only covering to the linoleum and on that smooth surface it slid easily through the gap.

A peep through the unobstructed leg of the keyhole showed her only the old man's hands. He seemed to be relaxed, as if sleeping again. She listened, but a faint sound of music prevented her from hearing whether his breathing was regular. She decided to burn her boats.

With the mat pushed out as far as it would stretch, she fiddled with her battered scrap of gold wire. The key was awkward and her wire lacked stiffness, but at last she managed to turn the key into the upright position and to push it out. The virtue of the mat over the more traditional sheet of newspaper was immediately obvious. She hardly heard the fall of the key, but when she pulled back the mat it was there under her hand.

Sylvia felt faintly sick. Passivity was past and she must take initiative for which she felt unready.

Somebody entered the kitchen and left it again. When she stooped to the keyhole all was silent again and she could see the old man asleep.

The chance of the moment might soon be gone. She turned the stiff lock and pulled the door open. The kitchen was empty except for the sleeper and silent except for the sound of far-off music. The window was high in the wall and barred. She left the key in the outside of the door.

The kitchen door stood half-open. She listened and then slipped through, to find herself in a short passage. To her right was a baize-covered door which opened against a spring when she pushed it. She saw a hallway, narrow but richly papered and carpeted, and an open door from which spilled the sound of voices and a background of Mozart. Beyond was the front door, inaccessible.

She let the baize-covered door close. Another door opposite the kitchen opened into a wine cellar, fully stocked. She turned the other way and climbed the stair down which Jimmy had carried her. At the top she found the back door of the house. Evidently the house was on a hill and the back lane was higher than the street. The door was bolted and locked, there was no key and the little window beside it was again barred.

At the other end of the passage was another baize door. Sylvia realised that she was on what had once been the back stair, leading up to the attics where the servants would once have had their bedrooms. Could she find a hiding place up there? But no. They would guess that she was still in the house. Also, the upper stair was in darkness and if she switched lights on she might give herself away.

She peeped through the baize door and saw a landing, as richly appointed as the hall below, the doors of what she supposed would be bedrooms and the head of another staircase leading down towards the hall. She could hear muffled voices again, but whether these came from the bedrooms or from the ground floor or both she could not guess.

Even if the upper windows were unbarred, she could not see herself climbing down the face of the building. If she prowled from room to room it would surely not be long before she met somebody; and in that house anybody might be an enemy.

With visitors coming and going, the front door would not be as obstructive as the back. A second or two should see it open and then she could slip into the darkness outside or, if pursuit were imminent, run screaming through the streets. It was that or return to her cell and trust to luck and the honourable intentions of her kidnappers.

She descended the back stair and looked through into the hall again. Nothing had changed. The front door seemed to be secured only by a latch and a Yale-type lock.

Tiptoeing along the hallway, she felt her own heart-beat and tried to find some spittle to moisten her mouth. The door to the occupied room was only partly open and screened most of the interior, but there was a wide gap at the hinged edge and she risked a quick look.

In a room which was luxurious from the deep carpet to the crystal chandelier, and enthroned in a Hepplewhite armchair with scrolled arms and feet, Doris Knight was presiding over a buffet supper. Two men were within Sylvia's view, although she could hear the voices of others, and they were fully dressed but the three visible girls were almost nude. (Sylvia's first thought on glimpsing the stockings and suspender-belts was not 'How shocking!' but 'How old-fashioned!') One of the girls, a dyed blonde, was tied securely to a chair but was placidly accepting the food which one of the men was feeding to her with a fork.

With that bizarre fragment etched on her mind Sylvia moved on quickly to the front door. The Yale-type latch was quickly turned and secured, but the door was also chained and the chain was attached to its own lock with a mechanism which she had not seen before. Each time that she thought that she had disengaged it, the chain remained obstinately fast.

A jingling behind her back cut short her tenth, fumbling attempt to free the door. She looked round. Two men in the black ties and tailcoats of waiters had wheeled a trolley laden with half-empty dishes out of the room where the festivities were in progress. One was large and one was small, and they reminded her of Laurel and Hardy until she saw that the ill temper in the larger man's face was not humorous but malevolent and that the smaller man was an albino.

Although they were moving towards her, the men had still not had time to digest Sylvia's sudden appearance. She, on the other hand, was already nerved for flight. She ducked under their outstretched arms and ran for the stairs, throwing herself upward in stumbling desperation. At the half-landing, she glanced down and saw the albino was coming after her but that the fat man was unhurriedly walking towards the baize-covered door and the back stairs.

Sylvia fled on and up, her footsteps silent on the heavy carpeting, past the first floor to the empty second. Her only thought now was to get back to the kitchen and lock herself into the safety of her little cell. The albino was half a flight behind her. She dived through the door which she knew must lead to the back stairs and began to descend through semi-darkness, her feet now clattering on the bare boards. She reached the baize door at first floor level before meeting the fat man. She could hear the albino somewhere behind her. She plunged through on to the front landing, hoping to reach the kitchen door by way of the front stairs while the two men were still above her.

She had been outguessed. A heavy arm clamped round her waist, lifting her off her feet and squeezing the breath out of her. The albino's feet clattered to the doorway behind her and then became silent. She was carried to one of the doors.

'In here?' said her captor's voice. It was high and fluting for such a large frame, and almost musical.

The albino appeared. He tried the door, looked inside and nodded.

'Go and get rid of that trolley before the guests come out, or your aunt'll do her nut.'

The albino nodded again and disappeared.

The fat man lifted Sylvia into the room and set her on her feet, shifting his grip to her hair. 'Scream if you want to,' he said. His breath was foul in her face. 'This place is pretty soundproof and screams are nothing new. We might even relish it.'

Sylvia was too busy recovering the breath which had been squeezed out of her to scream. She was aware of a room like a whore's boudoir, with a mirror on the ceiling and strange devices, and of the sweat glistening on the man's face.

The fat man shook her by the hair. 'You're not going to be raped, if that's what's worrying you,' he said. 'My friend and I don't go in for that sort of thing. We don't like girls very much. Not for sex. So you can stand by and watch while we enjoy each other. And then we'll get around to you.'

He began to tie knots in her long hair. She held herself still and wished that she could faint.

The albino came back. 'All done,' he said. 'We're off for the night.'

The fat man pushed Sylvia to the door and slammed it on her knotted hair. He locked the door and took the key away.

The tension in her scalp made it difficult to close her lids. Sylvia covered her eyes with her hands as the two figures frolicked beside the bed.

SEVENTEEN

Major Craythorne spent the night in an armchair beside the uncurtained window of the Cantors' living room, with a rug over his knees and the telephone, the radio and a pair of night-glasses by his hand. He slept for an hour at a time between shorter periods of looking out.

He snapped awake in the early dawn to find Sylvia's mother standing over him in a quilted dressing-gown, ghostly in the faint light that penetrated the window.

'I'm sorry,' she said. 'I didn't mean to wake you. I can't sleep. I was just going to make a cup of tea. Would you like one?'

He yawned and stretched. 'Very much,' he said. She went away and he heard the kettle being filled. He resumed his scrutiny of the world outside. In the unlikely eventuality that somebody was intended to watch the house from the common, now would be the time to position him. His own patrol would cover the common later, but the removal of the watcher could be handled with more discretion if they had seen him settle.

Mrs Cantor came back with tea and biscuits and sat near him. 'It's dreadful to think of Sylvia, somewhere out there,' she said.

'I know.'

'What are you watching for?'

'Anything unusual.'

'Could I help?'

She would be better for some occupation. 'Keep watch for me while I catch up with my sleep,' he said. 'Look out for anything in the least out of the ordinary. A vehicle which shouldn't go past, a man who goes onto the common and disappears, anything like that. Will you?'

'Yes, of course,' she said. She pulled up a chair beside his.

The major finished his tea and leaned back. He fell asleep immediately. Later, it seemed only minutes later, she shook his arm. He looked at his watch. Another hour had passed.

'You'll think me silly,' she said. 'But there was something which didn't seem quite right.'

'Tell me.'

'A man came walking up the road carrying a suitcase. He was well wrapped up so that I couldn't see him properly. It could have been that boy Chas Gowans but it could have been almost anybody. I lost sight of him when he disappeared behind those rhododendrons by our garden wall. He took longer than I expected to come out the other side and walk on.'

'How much longer?' the major asked.

'Perhaps half a minute.'

'Was he still carrying the suitcase?'

'Yes. But it seemed much lighter. He wasn't having to lean the other way so much.'

'Well done!' said the major.

'Have I helped?'

'Enormously.' He looked at his watch again. The sergeant-major would be placing his men about now. He picked up his radio. 'Heather?'

The voice came back instantly. 'Sir?'

'Somebody just passed the house. Did you see him?'

'Afraid not, sir.'

'Never mind. He may have left something between the wall and the rhododendrons. Have somebody take a look, would you?'

A little later, a large man in a peaked cap and grey overalls walked past. Craythorne recognised the sergeant-major.

'Sir?'

'Yes?'

'Small attaché case.'

'It could be almost anything,' the major said, 'but I suspect a bomb. The girl's quite likely to know things our man wouldn't want told to the police. If it's a bomb, it won't be armed yet. But it may be booby-trapped. The trap won't be set if there's a timer inside, but it might be if the thing's radio-controlled. I want somebody to uplift it and take it to the nearest bomb-disposal unit for X-raying. If it's not radio-controlled, I want it back where it was. If it is, take it away and lose it. Got that?'

'Sir.'

'And, sergeant-major, don't march around. Try to shuffle like a civilian.'

'I'll try very hard, sir.' He could hear the amusement in the sergeant-major's voice.

The major put down his radio. 'That's all right, then,' he said.

Sylvia's mother had found a new reserve of strength and calm. 'If it's a bomb,' she said, 'how can it be all right?'

'Because now he must operate close to here. Our big risk was that he'd set up a meeting in a hurry and a long way away from here. That way, he could make it impossible for my friends to stay on my tail and he could kill me and take the money without releasing Sylvia at all. But if he wants his bomb to catch Sylvia at home, he's got to make sure that home is where she's taken. Hand her over away from here and she could be taken tc make a statement to the police before she's brough home. And he wouldn't like that at all.'

'No, I don't suppose he would,' she said. She looked a him thoughtfully. 'Were you really prepared to take tha risk? For Sylvia?'

He laughed at her. 'We'll never know now, will we? He wouldn't be planting a bomb unless he was going to let me bring Sylvia home.'

She nodded as if he had answered her question. 'I'll go and see if my husband's awake,' she said. 'Poor dear, I don't know how he'll get through the day.'

The day ground along, hobbling like a very old man, without pace or future. Four watchers at road junctions and two on the common kept the major informed of a thousand movements, each of which was soon proved to be innocent. Before noon he saw the sergeant-major's figure, now in a dark boiler suit and a traffic warden's hat, slouch by. The bomb was back in place and the details of its construction were known to the whole team. He called one of the watchers on the common to come closer. The sky was like slate and he knew that the brisk wind would have a bite to it, but none of the men complained.

On the stroke of midday there was another phone call, again from a coin box. 'The family has two cars,' Chas said.

'That's right.'

'Do you have a car with you?'

'No.'

'Take Mr Cantor's Jag and park it at the near end of Rowan Lane. Then take Mrs Cantor's Sierra and leave it where Harmony Close joins the main road. Keep both sets of keys. And remember, any sign of the police and the girl dies,' Chas's voice added. He was almost shouting. The major decided that he was in a dangerous state.

'I say, I can't prevent a panda car going past on other business,' Craythorne said mildly.

'You better pray they don't,' Chas said.

He hung up. The major relayed the call over the radio.

'Does that change anything?' Mr Cantor asked.

'I don't think so. It just gives them two places to check for police watchers. They won't spot my men.'

Dusk arrived, the deepening gloom allowing the street lights to take over. Home-going traffic grew and then died away again. The major alerted himself. The man would move while the streets were quiet, either now or later in the night.

'Sir?' said the radio.

'Yes?'

'Henderson. Hatchback pulling into layby, man getting out.' There was a long pause. 'All clear. He only wanted a pee. He's driven off towards Brushton.'

And so it went on. Sylvia's mother brought the major food on a tray. Mr Cantor offered him wine, but he refused. Sleep was too close after his broken night.

'Sir?'

'Yes?'

'Wimpey van passing the house, going slow. Funny time and place for it.'

'I see him,' the major said. 'Driver alone in the front. Seemed to be having a good look around.'

'He's turning and coming back,' said another voice.

The van passed again. The pale blob of face could have been Chas or anybody. They waited. The Cantors were sitting dumbly on the couch. The major saw that they were holding hands and that Mr Cantor was gripping too hard.

'Wimpey van stopped outside post office. Young man gone into phone box. I could . . . '

'Do nothing,' the major snapped. 'He may not be alone.'

'You're right, sir. I can make out another man in the back.'

The phone rang. Before picking it up, he attached a sucker-microphone to the phone and plugged it into his radio.

After the usual coin box noises, the same voice came on. It sounded breathless with nerves, another danger sign. 'Is the money ready?'

'It's beside me now.'

'But you told the police.'

A bluff.

'The police know nothing about this. Nothing at all.'

'Good. If they turn up, the girl dies. You too, probably. Now listen. Count up to sixty and then move. Go out of the Cantors' front gate, carrying the money. Turn left. Walk. Keep taking the first left. You'll be met.'

The connection was broken. The major picked up the radio. 'Heather?'

'Sir?'

'You got that?'

'Loud and clear.'

'I think it's a ploy to see whether I'm followed. Cover me if you can but for God's sake don't be seen. Take no action whatever until the girl's safe. Out.'

Craythorne got to his feet. He was very stiff after a night and a day spent mostly sitting.

'Good luck!' Cantor said, and his wife added, 'Be careful.'

'I will. You'll have her back soon, I promise. And not a word to the police until we've discussed exactly what, if anything, is to be said. I don't want any of my men anded in trouble.'

'We understand.'

He shrugged on his coat and went out into the cold. The case was heavy.

He turned left and walked. After a few minutes he ame to a junction and turned into another road of rivate houses. The streets were empty but he saw the pale shape of a van tucked into shadows further along the road which he had left. Somebody was moving parallel to him through the gardens, but so quietly that he knew that it was one of his own men.

He made three more turns and found himself back in the Cantors' road. This time the van was backed into the mouth of a track on the common. He paid it no attention but he heard it begin to move behind him.

As he reached the Cantors' gate, the contractor's van – yellow, but looking paler under the street lamps – arrived from his right and braked to a rough halt beside him. Through the open, nearside window he could make out a girl's face and he recognised it as Sylvia's although the mouth was taped. There was something at her neck which he had difficulty making out . . . a hand from the back, that was it, holding a knife against her throat. Her eyes were bright with fear.

A man with a beard – surely a false beard – leaned across from the driver's seat. 'Put the money through the window,' he said. It was the voice from the telephone.

The major lifted the suitcase and tried. 'It won't go through the window,' he said. 'It's too big.'

'Slide the door open. Don't try anything or we'll get blood all over us.'

As the door slid back he saw that Sylvia's wrists were cuffed in front of her and her ankles were tied. He passed the suitcase across her body. He could tell that she recognised him. She even managed to smile with her eyes. 'Don't worry,' he told her. 'You'll be home in a minute.'

She nodded.

The man in the driver's seat opened the case and checked through the money. It seemed to take a year and more. The major stood and spoke comfortingly under his breath to the girl. Suddenly the driver closed the case and passed it back over his shoulder. The knife vanished

The man put his hand on Sylvia's side to push her out.

'The key of the handcuffs,' Craythorne said quickly.

Chas hesitated and then fished the key out of his pocket and threw it past Craythorne's head. Sylvia was thrust out roughly and the major found himself holding her in his arms while the van accelerated heavily away.

The key was lying on the path. He managed to grab it up without dropping Sylvia and hurried to the house.

EIGHTEEEN

Around two corners, Chas braked the van to another halt. 'Wait here,' he said. 'Shan't be a minute.'

'Where you going?' the bruiser demanded, but he was too late. Chas had gone. The bruiser decided that it didn't matter. After all, he was holding the money.

Less than a minute later, the door slid open. When, instead of Chas, he saw a man in a traffic warden's hat, the bruiser still saw no cause for alarm. When a back-handed blow with a knuckleduster laid him out, he saw nothing at all.

Much later, he came to his senses. His face was swollen and he had lost three teeth. He found that he was in the local graveyard, lying in the bottom of a grave which had been opened for a funeral on the morrow. A wreath from another grave had been laid on his chest.

He took the hint and set off for home.

Chas Gowans leaned over the low garden wall. The movement made little points of light dance in front of his eyes as the blood rushed back to his drug-starved brain, but the right movements seemed to come to him as if from Heaven. Perhaps somebody was on his side after all.

A small bird rustling in the bushes made his nerves jump. He stopped and listened but there was nobody within sight or sound.

Detonator into primer. Wires on to spade terminals Give the timer a twist and hear the ticking start. Threa the string through the hole. Close the attaché case an snap the locks. Pull the string. All set. The case would go up. If it were opened it would go up sooner, that was all.

He picked the case up, very gently. Tiptoe up the path and hide the case among the clematis beside the door, and hey for his new passport and foreign parts.

He had been alone in the street when he started his work. When his wrist was seized, his heart nearly stopped and he made a small whinnying sound. He recognised the man. It was only Craythorne, the sissy.

'Fuck off,' Chas said. 'I got the girl back for you, didn't I? What more do you want from me?'

'Did you?' Craythorne said. Chas felt something out of place and looked down. A pair of handcuffs – they looked like the ones which the girl had been wearing – had been snapped onto his wrist and onto the handle of the case. 'I want nothing more from you,' Craythorne said. 'You can run along now.'

'But . . . '

'Is it the key of the handcuffs you want? I don't have it. Look over the road. There's a path leading across the common. In the middle of the common there's a war memorial. The key's at the foot of it. I should hurry, if I were you. You've got just as long as you gave yourself.'

In a spasm of rage, Chas raised the attaché case as if to hit the other with it. He could blast the man to kingdom come and never mind if he went along for the ride. But his instinct for self-preservation took over. He lashed out needlessly with his other hand, missed, used the free energy to spin on his heel and bolted across the road.

Craythorne mopped his forehead with a shaking hand. For a moment, he had known real fear. The man was mad enough to have swung the case at him, and then God alone knew what would have happened. Nothing, probably. The boffins had reported that the bomb was exceptionally well made. They could even make a guess at the hand which had made it.

He pulled himself together and took the radio out of his pocket. 'Scarper,' he said. 'I repeat, scarper.'

Chas stumbled along the path. As he moved away from the street the light faded until he was moving through almost total darkness. How the hell was he supposed to find the key in this? Bushes grabbed at his clothes and swung him aside.

The path forked. Craythorne had said nothing about this. He took what seemed to be the wider path and hurried on. His heart pounded in his chest like a pile driver. The case weighed a ton. He had banged it about enough, perhaps he had shaken the wires off the terminals. Christ, his knees felt as soft as cotton wool!

Now the path seemed to be petering out into an open space. He knelt down, hoping to see the war memorial against the glow of the town, but there was nothing but the silhouettes of trees.

In desperation, he knelt on the case and pulled with all his strength against the handcuff until it seemed as if the pressure would burst his head like an overblown balloon, but the handle refused to come away from the case.

Surely the time must be more than up by now? He had only given the dial the smallest twist. If the clock had stopped, perhaps he could go back to the house and ask the man Craythorne for directions.

No.

He got up and ran again, only to stumble in a rabbit hole and fall flat. The case came down with a thump. He took a moment out of his dwindling store to recover his breath.

Perhaps he was not meant to die. They had known that the case was there, or why would the man have been waiting? Perhaps they had disarmed it in some way. Perhaps it was all some hideous practical joke and they were laughing their heads off while he crashed around i the darkness, sobbing with fear.

Well, he'd have the last laugh. He got to his knees and fumbled for the latches in the darkness.

Sergeant-Major Heather came out of the rhododendrons with the other case in his hand. The two soldiers were standing together when the instant of light flared over the common. A second later the detonation reached them.

'Hope he didn't damage the war memorial,' Heather said. 'Can't have young squirts like that going around blowing up memorials to our gallant dead.'

'There isn't a war memorial,' the major said. In his pocket his hand closed over the handcuff key. 'Give me your torch. I'll see if I can't recover those handcuffs before the civil authorities make an appearance.'

The tape had been soaked away from Sylvia's mouth but she was still silent, not wholly from shock but because she did not know what to say to these people, these almost-strangers, her parents, who seemed to have moved heaven and earth for her. Her mother supported her upstairs and undressed her as if she were still a baby, suppressing a gasp when she saw the extent of the bruising.

'Come on, darling,' Mrs Cantor said. 'I'm going to give you a hot bath and then you can have a milky drink and go off to sleep in your own bed.' She put a dressing-gown around her daughter's shoulders and went to run hot water. She felt the shock of the explosion on the common, but her thoughts were with Sylvia. The girl had said nothing since that young man had brought her to the door. It would be better if she cried or swore or talked it out, anything but this zombie-like compliance.

Sylvia stood where her mother had left her. She wanted a bath. God, how she wanted a bath! But it was too much trouble. The awful things had stopped happening, better times had resumed. Let them happen to her without requiring conscious thought. She had no thoughts or emotions left to expend.

Her mother returned. 'Come along, darling,' she said brightly. 'We'll clean you up and you can get some sleep. You don't have to do anything or see anyone yet, and you can sleep late in the morning.' It was as if they had gone back to nursery days, infinitely comforting.

Sylvia stirred and her cracked lips parted. Her mother had to lean close to hear the tiny voice. 'Oh Mummy! I wish you'd stop fussing.'

Mrs Cantor blinked back the tears of joy. Her little girl was back.